EDITION TWO:
TRAM NUMBER TWO
(And a passing reference to tram number eight)

A novel

By

Charles J Bunyan

Author's Note

In the English speaking world, the name John Smith would excite no comment and in the German speaking world, the name Hans Schmidt would excite no comment.

In the Spanish speaking world, the name Jesus Maria Magdalena Peron would excite no comment. But when a man having that name suffers cultural displacement and moves to Berlin and then Amsterdam, he wearies of the puerile jokes of ignorant people who are not of the Spanish world. He begins to use the religious metaphor and analogy to describe phases in his life as a defensive mechanism.

Forsaking a brilliant career as a doctor in Berlin he takes up residence in Amsterdam and begins a new career as an international drug smuggler where his use of the religious metaphor has disquieting consequences for the authorities there...

Among all the "black" humour in this novel, there are, I hope, some serious points being made about the drug policies of governments and the differing treatment of social classes before the law.

CHAPTER ONE
In which Rudi, the German drug dealer, describes Jesus Peron, the head of an international drug ring.

Jesus was the most complex man I ever encountered. That said, he could at one and the same time appear to be endearingly simple. In his own words he had two religions and practised both. He saw no inherent contradiction in this, pointing out that it was quite common for Chinese people to have two religions, for example Buddhism and Taoism. It could be said, he argued with some humour, that Chinese people have three religions, Buddhism, Taoism and Communism, assuming the latter could be regarded as a religion!
Jesus was a practising Roman Catholic and Communist with an all-consuming hatred of the Americans and the British. The reason for his hatred was the appalling ill-treatment his peasant family had endured in the country of his birth.
He felt it was grotesquely unjust that peasants should be punished for their cultural heritage which includes the use of drugs for medicinal purposes and as a means of augmenting their miserable incomes.
He was always quick to point out the drug dealing activities of the Americans in Laos, Vietnam, Cambodia and The Bekka Valley and elsewhere and never let us forget the suitcases of heroin on board the Pan-American Jumbo downed over Lockerbie in Scotland in 1988. As for the British, there were the opium wars with China. Need one say more?

Flamboyantly clever and a qualified doctor in Berlin by the age of twenty-one, he was by turns urbane, sophisticated, civilised and witty and by turns brutally violent, insensitive to the needs and feelings of others and simplistic.

His full name was Jesus Maria Magdalena Peron. His family had moved to Berlin in 1990 when he was still a child and his name caused much mirth among the ignorant children of the school he was sent to. Ignorance he defined as people who did not speak Spanish or understand their customs and culture. Jesus is pronounced "Heyzuss" in the Spanish tongue and is frequently given to a male child. Wearying of the endless harassment he endured at school over his name, Jesus frequently alluded to aspects of his criminal career with New Testament analogies of The Saviour's life but only in the company of intimate associates and friends. Thus when he was found by the Berlin police at the age of 14 to be dispensing cocaine and other drugs to addicts outside the church known to Berliners as "the powder box and the lipstick", he likened it to his New Testament's namesake conversing with the learned men in the Temple at the same age in that the episode displayed his precocious talents in drug dealing.

Jesus removed to Amsterdam at the age of 30 there to begin his drug trafficking career proper describing this as the start of his "public ministry". He was six feet two inches in height, slim, had a full head of jet black hair, a dark sallow complexion and large brown eyes mostly twinkling with amusement except when aroused by adversity when they turned to the psychopathically emotionless eyes of a cobra snake.

His dress sense left much to be desired. Mostly he attired himself in what he considered to be "revolutionary chic"-army fatigues, boots and a green army baseball hat. For his musical street gigs he wore the same but with a red hat on his head. He wore a black suit for business meetings. As regards the former mode of dress, it gave him the appearance of a latter-day Che. He answered criticism of the first mode of dress by pointing out that wealthy Chinese dressed in "revolutionary chic" that is in black jackets and Mao caps. As regards criticism of the second mode of dress his answer was that he was after all, a "businessman" and a black suit was entirely appropriate. I shall explain shortly why he often wore a red hat for his street gigs.

Jesus Maria Magdalena Peron was not a man to trifle with and was a sight to behold when aroused. On one occasion he asked me as a matter of supreme urgency to attend at the police station in Marystraat. As a trusted lieutenant I went there immediately and upon arrival encountered a scene which would not have been amiss in a Wild West film except that instead of horses tied up outside a saloon bar there were a Maserati (his favourite mode of conveyance) and a number of BMWs belonging to his gang—littering the pavement which the Cafe des Amis shared with the police station there. Various tough looking South American thugs were gathered outside the police station fingering their guns. I enquired of Jesus what the reason for the summons was. He replied that he had been informed that the police were "torturing" one of his men. I indicated that I was somewhat slower on the draw than the famous American actor Clint Eastwood and was in consequence whereof unlikely to be of much assistance to him in the forthcoming resolution of matters. Mercifully the matter was resolved without bloodshed.

Every story, they say has a beginning, a middle and an end. I shall not depart from the structure contained in this platitudinous observation and shall therefore begin with a brief account of my own early life and then an account of my first meeting with Jesus. Thereafter I shall describe his associates and activities as best I can.
Before I do so it is appropriate to expound my own views on drugs.
My readers (ranging from officials of the American and British governments to the police of Amsterdam) will be anxious no doubt to discover my views on drugs. I am happy to supply that information. My clinical dissection and irrefutable analysis of the subject will not make me popular. I do not care.
The first matter to notice is this: the psycho-babble of modern psychology dictates that altered states of consciousness are bad for us. What poppy-cock (forgive the horticultural pun). The psychologists who peddle such nonsense are either the very same psychologists or have colleagues who are happy to advise their British and American governments on how to torture anyone who opposes them with psychotropic drugs. As regards practitioners of

psychology who work for governments, I can think of no profession which more richly deserves the hangman's noose. If only Nuremburg could be reconvened for them and the death penalty imposed. (There were "Doctors trials" at Nuremburg—the worst offenders were hanged.)

The second matter to notice is that we human beings throughout recorded history have greatly enjoyed our state of consciousness being altered. The Ancient Egyptians smoked hashish. In more modern times Victorian England barely functioned without laudanum and members of the ruling classes of Great Britain were never averse to a decanter of malt whisky.

In my view a fundamental truth was enunciated by the Maharishi Mahesh Yogi who propounded the view that the mind had to have a place where it was happy to go. Transcendental meditation can lead to pure consciousness or, preferably the highest state of consciousness, God consciousness. Few human beings ever achieve that state.

The descendants of Freud advise no states of altered consciousness and in its place advocate sex! Words almost fail me! Sex releases three different classes of amphetamine and morphine in the body!

In conclusion, if you command even a basic grasp of history, then the conduct of British and American governments in the field of drug-trafficking will truly shock you. Serious academic studies have proven that historically that they were the biggest drug pedlars of all.

CHAPTER TWO
In which Rudi, the German drug dealer, describes his early life.

A "drug mule" is, of course, a person who smuggles drugs on behalf of drug cartels for money.
Those who work for the Columbian and Bolivian cartels are well-paid if things go well and normally deliver consignments to Spain, France, the UK and Germany or elsewhere. What they do is dangerous work. If they "betray" such organisation even in some minor way the tendons in their hands and arms will be slit, making it impossible for them to urinate or defecate and clean themselves afterwards. This makes for a lifetime of misery and humiliation. Those who commit more serious transgressions suffer fates which I shall leave to the imagination.
Captain Jan Van P... of the Amsterdam Police, on behalf of his government and others, has offered me a lesser sentence if I will "co-operate". I have decided to do so but with my heart in my mouth. What I am about to do will almost certainly result in my departure from this life, witness protection schemes or no.
I shall now sketch in my early life.
I was born in and spent the earlier part of my life in Rudesheim on The Rhine. Like so many of Rhineland youth I was washed down the Rhineland gorge.

My earlier life, in my submission, has no relevance to this major drug trafficking enquiry and I shall be brief. I am thirty-seven years of age.

My childhood and youth were happy save the minor and normal upsets of adolescence. My parents owned (and almost single-handedly) ran a small hotel with something of a view of the Rhine. From an early age therefore I had, by force of circumstances, been compelled to suffer the endless intrusions of hotel guests and the older I became, the more irksome it was.

It may not appear to be a position that attracts much sympathy but I grew to yearn for escape from what was superficially a tourist and vineyard idyll. (Indeed by my late teens I eschewed wine (even the most distinguished vintages) in favour of beer. I was in my late twenties before I could face consuming wine again except on an intermittent basis.)

Escape I did in my eighteenth year. God, Providence or genetics (take your pick according to your persuasions) had endowed me with a gift for music. I had the highest grades in violin, piano and guitar and literally walked into what was then The *Staatliche Hochschule fur Musik*. God, I was happy there! No more tourists telling me to stop making such a "noise" on my instruments; no more renditions of *Lorelei* and no more guests becoming inebriated on bottles of wine desperately trying to come up with a business plan to own a small vineyard on The Rhine!

In Cologne I studied and played by day. By night I played in a group of fellow students down by The Rhine. We often made good money!

Gifted musically I may have been, but then God is not miserly in his scattering of musical gifts among humanity. Frankly, whatever my gifts, I was not destined for world acclaim and as with so many others before me, one day I had to apply my mind to earning a living. It is, as any student knows, a most sobering experience. In student life a gifted person perceives that he or she has been blessed by God and then, one day, "reality" intrudes.
Whatever the gifts, you must make a living. It is as simple and brutal as that. Again, as with many others, I was forced to consider the appalling fate of having to teach in order to eat, be clothed and housed.
Teach I did-by day-and at night I played in any musical group who would have me. In that way I kept my sanity. In the same way as the magnificent River Rhine eventually prostitutes itself and dissipates in The Netherlands and The North Sea, I eventually ended up in The Netherlands. That is I went to live in Amsterdam, to be precise. Yes, I am aware that what remains of the River Rhine, by the time it enters the soil of The Netherlands, does so some miles from Amsterdam but I can surely be forgiven for some geographical latitude in my allegorical comparison!

CHAPTER THREE
In which Rudi, the German drug dealer, meets Jesus in Amsterdam and is "reborn".

And it was in Amsterdam that, as the old song has it, fate lent a hand. I encountered Jesus. It happened thus.
The first time I saw him was in *The Leidseplein* in Amsterdam wearing what I soon discovered was his trademark red hat. He wore this as a symbol of his support for the terrorist, Maoist "The Shining Path" of Peru. Well, that is how the CIA described them and international communism in general. He was attired in army "fatigues" and had a Havana cigar jammed between his teeth. He was in the company of his Peruvian wind pipe band playing "Guantanamera." This is always a popular ditty with tourists anywhere despite the chilling thought of the American Belsen there.
May I here give a word of explanation for any of my readers who are unfamiliar with Amsterdam or the Leidseplein. I must confess that in any other capital city in the world (especially Germany) the Leidseplein would be written off as an abomination or, to use a German word, "kitsch". Somehow Amsterdam gets away with it. Those of a precise, geometrical bent will immediately query the use of the word "Square" to describe Leidseplein but let's not get too technical. The Square lies on the intersection of tram routes.
All roads lead to Rome. Well that may have been true once-upon-a-time for The Eternal City. But in

Amsterdam for Jesus Maria Magdalena Peron, and my good self, all roads (or rather trams) led to the Leidseplein. It was after all the intersection of many tram routes in the city and an ideal conduit for the distribution of drugs throughout the city.

There are numerous bars in the Square with outside seating (very important for the last remaining "puffers" or smokers left on the planet) and normally a plethora of street musicians are in attendance to satisfy the musical needs of the customers. In winter time, there is an ice rink. I prefer the summer, needless to say.

Eventually Jesus took a break from his mighty musical endeavours with the Peruvian band and grabbed a Heineken beer to assuage the thirst which rendition of the various South American dittys had occasioned and sat down at my table.

"*Hola, Senor,*" he said good-naturedly, conveying the beer to his lips with one hand and tipping his red hat back on his head with other. A darkly good-looking girl who looked quite fetching in what I took to be native Peruvian garb sat down on the remaining seat at the table.

Jesus noticed my appraising look.

"*Te gusta la Mujer?*" he enquired in familiar South American Spanish. You like the woman? He sounded like an attentive shop assistant enquiring of a customer as to whether the merchandise met with my approval.

There was little point in anything but honesty.

"She is breathtaking," I replied as if *La Mujer* was not there, or at least, some sort of slave girl to be inspected.

"*Bonita*," I added shamelessly. Beautiful. Indeed she was. And the right colour scheme for me. She was dressed in a poncho and jeans and appeared to be in no way incommoded by the frank inspection of her person which *Jesus* had invited. So far as I could tell she viewed the entire proceedings as entirely normal behaviour by a male. Well, by a male from Peru at any rate.

Jesus initially gave me the impression that he was quite prepared to share his women-beautiful or not-with men who met with his approval. I was wrong and will shortly explain why. Clearly, though, he had taken a liking to me for whatever reason. Having finished his beer he announced that he was about to recommence playing with his band.

"I have some more tunes to play for these good people," and here he gestured at the many souls populating the Leidseplein.

"I shall be through in some minutes and then you must join me at The Uruguayan Steakhouse just off The Square. *La Mujer* will come with us."

La Mujer once more did not appear incommoded by the turn of events.

Before Jesus could strike up the band again, a rowdy incident took place.

Now and again the peace of The Netherlands was disturbed by those most disruptive people, the British. Why of why must they spoil everyone's peace? That night in the Leidseplein it was, of course, members of The British Army on "a night out". What pigs! They had had far too much to drink and wanted to sing "God Save the Queen" in order to incommode Jesus and his musicians. Why behave in that manner? In my opinion it is because their soldiers are working-class thugs. They are then given the opportunity to carry on their working-class thuggery by another means namely in the army. (I paraphrase Clausewitz.) The British Army (as it has been throughout its Imperial history) is run by the ruling elite and these thugs from the lower orders prop up the ghastly scum who rule the British. That night, in The Square of the Leidseplein, the outcome of their disruptive behaviour was truly amusing. The soldiers were no match for Jesus and his band of wandering minstrels (all of whom were black belts in various martial arts disciplines.)

Later The British Army thugs were to complain loudly about Peruvian "thugs"! It was to no avail. The Amsterdam Courts would not listen and they were deported forthwith.

After this fracas it was off to the Uruguayan steakhouse off the Leidseplein minus the British Army thugs who were left on the square bleeding from their numerous wounds and, in some cases, attempting to save "God Save The Queen".

The name of *La Mujer* was Concepcion and she was twenty three years of age. I swiftly discovered the reason why Jesus had not taken any offence by my casting a shameless appraising eye over her. Her second name was Peron and she was a first cousin of Jesus.

Concepcion should have been the fulfilment of the two middle names of Jesus but she was not. Their relationship was deeply loving but asexual.

During dinner while my host relived the minutiae of the recent combat in The Square with his "troops" and consumed a large portion of a dead animal (described enthusiastically in the menu as "The Works"), I was left to ingratiate myself with his first cousin in any way I could.

Her parents I gleaned from this strikingly attractive girl had not been motivated by any religious concerns when giving her the name Concepcion. It is a common name for a girl in the Spanish world. Nor, in so naming her, were her progenitors expressing some hope that their daughter would prove productive in her child-bearing years. Far from it, the name Concepcion for a Spanish girl is meant to indicate "purity" although how such a virtue was to be divined as early as christening was beyond my powers of rational analysis.

"So when did you arrive from Peru?" I ventured.
"Twenty three years ago, in my mother's womb."
"Here, in the Netherlands?"
She laughed.
"No, my parents and the parents of Jesus all arrived as a large family group in Germany in 1990. The Berlin Wall had come down. There were many business opportunities in the city and they had the chance to set up in there."
"A restaurant, I suppose?"
"Of course."
"So you are German?"
"Of course. That's where I was born."
I allowed myself a few seconds to digest this information. To be candid, and perhaps because I came from and spent my early and teenage years in Rudesheim, I had difficulty adjusting to the multracial aspects of the modern Germany. Well do I recall the first occasion when I encountered fluent

black Germans in Cologne. Ah, the difficulties we rural, country folk from Rudesheim have in coming to terms with modern German life!

"So your school years were spent in Berlin?"

"Yes but I did not wholly enjoy them."

"Why?"

"Too many foreigners in the area of the city we lived in," she replied without a hint of irony.

"There are too many Turks, Poles and Russians."

It was best to make no comment on that matter.

"So how did you end up in the band with Jesus?"

"We have always been close and I knew he had started a business in Amsterdam..."

"What kind of business?"

"You ask so many questions!"

"I apologise. As you may have gathered, you interest me."

"Jesus!" she called to her cousin.

"Concepcion!".

"This man wants to know what you do for a living."

"Is he a policeman?"

"I don't know. Are you a policeman?"

"No, I am a musician."

"That's alright then. You may tell him I import large quantities of cocaine from my brothers in Peru," he shouted.

Everyone laughed. Only later did I discover that he spoke the truth.

"What music do you play Senor?"

"Almost anything that can be played on a violin, guitar or piano."

Ah Concepcion! It was as if God had breathed her into existence. I regard myself as both educated and articulate. That said I find it impossible to summon the words to adequately describe her. I have already referred to her in this statement as "strikingly" good looking and "breathtakingly" attractive. I am struck by the poverty of the adjectives I have been able to muster.

Let me paint a picture of her as best I can. She had black hair that tumbled to her shoulders and was possessed of a finely sculpted face in the Spanish way, out of which flashed two large and expressive brown-black eyes. If eyes mirror the soul then hers was revealed as a warm and compassionate. At twenty three she was slim without a trace of the many extra grams which so many young women seem to carry nowadays and somehow wore the South American clothes elegantly and without a trace of pretension or affectation. The jewellery she wore was always discreet and expensive. "Bling"- the means by which women nowadays hope to convince the undiscerning male of an extrovert personality with a hint of promiscuity-was never on display. Bling after all is cheap and makes a woman look cheap.

Her speech was precise and she had a physical presence and intellect which intimidated all other women.

My efforts to describe her still strike me as miserably inadequate. Perhaps I can best encapsulate my description of her by saying that the totality of her physical and mental attributes combined to make all other women she encountered of whatever social strata or education feel deeply uneasy and look clumsy. None could hope to compete with her and they realised this.

18

It follows from what I have said that I was, to use the conventional phrase to describe such a condition, "in love" although I have never heard a satisfactory definition of the condition. My feelings for her led to my full-time employment in the organisation set up by Jesus and it is essential to grasp the importance of her contribution to it.

CHAPTER FOUR
In which Rudi, the German drug dealer describes the business enterprises of Jesus.

What with the band leader being called Jesus, the band itself being called The Twelve Apostles and Jesus having a first cousin called Concepcion, an outsider or The Amsterdam Police, had they known about us back then, might have concluded that we were some sort of religious cult or Jesus freaks. Such a superficial observation would have been confirmed by the fact that one of Jesus's many business enterprises was a music shop two tram stops further on from the Leidseplein which enjoyed the name "The Apostolic Sea".
The music shop was of course simply one of many business fronts to launder money. My interrogators are understandably keen to acquaint themselves with as much detail as possible about this aspect of our organisation.
The music shop which Jesus owned (one of his many entrepreneurial enterprises in the city) was exactly what you would expect of such an outlandish, larger than life person as he. Jesus being Jesus had bought a shop on the most expensive shopping street in Amsterdam, the P.C. Hoofstraat. That's along from The Concertgebouw if you don't know. It is usually described by the tourist office people as "The Fifth Avenue" of Amsterdam and is home to Gucci, Chanel, Louis Vuitton, Hilfiger and Ferrugamo among others.

He had one musical instrument in the shop window. It was a Bosendorfer Grand. (Jesus had decided that Steinways were too "common".) On the stool for the Grand, Jesus being Jesus had placed a hand-written Note which read:-
"This is a very expensive shop: if you don't have any money or a high disposable income or high net worth please do not enter these premises and waste my time".
Now there are two points to make about such a sales tactic. Firstly, that part of Amsterdam is expensive (a point Jesus emphasised by always leaving his Maserati parked outside the shop door) and secondly such a tactic was a direct challenge to the wealthy snobbish Amsterdamers who live in the vicinity. Such a rude, offensive and challenging notice in the shop window ensured Jesus was never short of customers.
En passant, I should tell you the story Jesus told me when explaining his decision to place a Bosendorfer Grand in the shop window.
He recounted how he had once been walking down Madison Avenue in New York and passed a ladies shoe shop. Now, if you don't know, Madison Avenue, New York is a posh area to shop. The shoe shop, Jesus said, had a front window display consisting of one single pair of ladies high heels. There was nothing as vulgar as a price tag affixed to the shoes. The price of the shoes was several thousand dollars as Jesus found out when he sauntered in to enquire. (In Madison Avenue you are presumed to have so much money that you do not require to ask the price). That shop display, Jesus said, made a statement.

He had also passed another shop window in Madison Avenue which sold paintings but the window was completely blacked out and displayed only a notice that prospective customers should pop their bank balance details through the letter box and assuming a check revealed that the prospective customer had several millions at the credit of his account, then admission would be allowed upon an appointment being made. So you can understand why Jesus had shoved a Bosendorfer Grand in his shop window with a rude notice on the stool pointing out that poor people need not enter.

The interior of the shop was no less intimidating for the poor. There were, to give but one example, two Strads in a display case with another rude notice hand written by Jesus.

This read:-

"If you have to ask the price of these violins then you cannot afford them."

In the shop, Jesus in his red hat and Concepcion-invariably attired in her Peruvian poncho ruled the roost as one might expect. There were two sales assistants rejoicing in the name of Consuela and Maria who were allowed to deal with "minor" purchases. A "minor purchase" was defined as musical instruments costing less than three thousand Euros (of which there were very few.)

Another front for laundering money was a coffee house just off Dam Square and near the Royal Palace. As my interrogators will know, it was not built as such originally but as the Town Hall and a rather splendid one at that. It shows you just how much money was made in the days of the Dutch

Empire from slavery, exploitation of subject peoples and the robbery of natural resources of their countries. Why people go on about drug dealers I do not know. I think we are morally superior to the "heroes" of anyone's Empire. Anyway The Cafe Grass did a roaring trade in cannabis products mainly to foreign tourists. In "coffee shops" foreign tourists behave like children in a sweet shop. They arrive at the airport, take the train into town, dump their bags at whatever hotel they are staying at, make a beeline for the coffee shops and excitedly examine the "menu". I never weary of looking at these silly children. As I write this statement the halcyon days of the coffee shops open to all may be coming to an end. There are moves afoot to stop coffee shops selling to anyone but Dutch citizens and residents. You do not need to be a genius to guess that fake identity cards will soon be a burgeoning business.

The other main business enterprise which Jesus ran was a fast food restaurant again just off Dam Square. Hundreds of people a day patronised this place unaware of the fact that every last one of them was helping to launder the profits of our organisation.

For completeness I should point out that Jesus was both a patron of the Arts and a generous patron of various charities in the city. As regards the former I would venture to suggest that if the staff of The Hermitage did not sight Jesus for a day or two, they would report him as a missing person to the police. As regards the latter, it is quite astounding how authorities will turn the proverbial blind eye to any financial irregularities if the person suspected of such irregularities was a well known benefactor of good causes.

CHAPTER FIVE
In which Rudi, the German drug dealer, explains the importance of Tram Number Two and Jesus refers to Tram Number Eight and gives his views on Europe.

Tram number two was, as I have said, the main conduit for Jesus's operations in Amsterdam. He was The Big Boss Man of the whole scene as some of our mules referred to him as.

The Number two tram route was the main artery for our consignments in the city. The route runs from Centraal Station via Leidseplein and Hoofdorpplein to Nieuw Sloten and stops at Marystraat which was where Jesus had a residence. It was situated in a reasonably affluent district of the city near The Vondel Park and, apart from some very acceptable apartments and houses in the vicinity, boasts an establishment called "The Cafe des Amis" a restaurant and bar which gives a good view of a police station that must prior, to its conversion to a pig pen, have been a pleasant and commodious house. It amused Jesus no end to superintend the transfer and distribution from his residence of pure cocaine and the like worth many millions of Euros across the road from the pig pen. It was at the Cafe des Amis one morning when we were having a coffee break that Jesus gave me the benefit of his views on the last seventy-five years or so of European history or at least a part of that history.

"Being a person who has suffered cultural displacement," he began, "I always make it my business to acquaint myself with a little of the history of whatever European country I am in. That way I don't feel so alien or strange. I then know something of the people and the country and can try to understand them and their ways. Now take the country we are in just now, The Kingdom of The Netherlands, to give the place its full title. What do you know about the place and its people?"
"Rembrandt, dykes of the water resistant variety, bicycles, tulips, cannabis, cheese, canals and Van Gogh. That's about the limit of my understanding of the place," I replied shamelessly.
Jesus shook his head in sorrow.
"Do you not even know that during "The Golden Age" as they call it, Holland was the dominant power in Europe and perhaps the world and ruled an Empire?"
"Vaguely," I replied with some embarrassment.
Tram Number Two rattled by.
"That's a tram," Jesus said.
"I think I have seen trams before."
"But did you know about the pivotal part that trams played in the history of this land recently?"
"No. Tell me about it."
"OK. Firstly tell me where Tram Number Eight goes to."
"Tram Number Eight?" I asked hesitantly. "I'm not sure..."
"There is no Tram Number Eight, Rudi, at least not in recent times. There was a Tram Number Eight when the Germans were here some seventy years ago. The route encompassed the various

Jewish quarters in the city and was put to use in ferrying the Jews to Centraal Station. Over a one hundred thousand disappeared. Like everyone else in Europe the Dutch decided to take shelter behind a collective amnesia. Do you know who said that?"
"No."
"Hans-Magnus Enzensberger. Do you know who he is?"
"No."
"Do you know anything?"
"Not much it seems."
"Anyway, the Dutch managed to forget about Tram Number Eight and about the twenty-three thousand who joined the Waffen SS. Amnesia is a wonderful thing. It allowed the Dutch-just like the French-to "remember" that they had all, to the last man and woman, been resistance fighters."
"Try not to be too hard on people. All nations have perpetrated dreadful acts of cruelty. Even the Israelis," I added lamely.
Jesus snorted at the mention of the Israelis.
"Whatever bestial acts were committed by Europeans, the Israelis have tried hard to emulate them. Ever heard of a guy called Vanunu?"
"No."
"He is a scientist who spent twenty years of his life in solitary confinement in Israel for revealing that they had four hundred nuclear bombs."
"The Israelis say that their policy is one of "nuclear ambivalence"."
Jesus let out a loud guffaw.
"Rudi, my child, there is fuck all ambivalent about having four hundred nukes."

"What of modern Europe?" I asked. "Surely you recognise what has been achieved?"
"Of course but everything that has been achieved has been achieved on the back of collective amnesia and the grant of universal absolution. Nothing can change the fact that Europe and its peoples stink from the Urals to the Atlantic Ocean."
"Thanks for your views," I said humorously, "but you have forgotten about the British."
"No I haven't, and don't get me started on those bastards. Let's get back to some decent drug peddling."
In conclusion I should add that for Jesus and I Tram Number Two was a bit like Tram Number Eight seventy years ago. It was where we conducted our filthy business and hoped that no-one would notice. But of course they did and that is why it was necessary to buy the silence and "blindness" of the tram conductor we encountered the most in the conduct of our business affairs. He was called Jacob and was almost seventy years old. Proof, I suppose, that the tram company did not discriminate against employees on grounds of age. Somewhat sadistically Jesus once pointed out that his oldest recruit was grateful on a daily basis to get away from Centraal Station on tram Number Two because he feared encountering a ghostly reincarnation of Tram Number Eight. Jesus could be cruel.

CHAPTER SIX
In which Rudi, the German drug dealer describes Jesus in his "church."

Now Jesus was a religious man but certainly not in any conventional sense of the word. He admired The Borgias and their ways. As with many religious men he saw no inherent contradiction between his religious beliefs and his criminal and occasionally murderous activities in the international drugs trade. Seeing no contradiction between the two would have made him an ideal companion for the likes of George Bush or Tony Blair, Winston Churchill or the common soldier.
And yet some of the love of God paradoxically oozed out of Jesus in his dealings with his family and intimates. That love of God did not extend to repentance for his "sins" of drug trafficking and nor did it mean the love of his enemies who, invariably, were killed on the slightest pretext.
As office premises Jesus had purchased The Church of The Doubting Thomas, Prinzen Gracht, Amsterdam, Kingdom of The Netherlands, and converted it into office space. This former church in the middle of Amsterdam served as Global Headquarters for The International Corporation for Fair Trade in Medical Products that is, our drug-trafficking headquarters.
The High Altar was now resplendent with several of the latest flat screens showing the latest position of our mules in the field and those who were considered to be traitors and marked down for

execution. It was where our business meetings were held. These meetings with "The Twelve Apostles" bore some resemblance to Da Vinci's Last Supper except that round the altar it was not the disciples of The New Testament who gathered but rather his most trusted South American hoodlums. On his orders they laid their weapons (usually Glocks) on the altar while they were in conference with "The Almighty", that is Jesus Peron.

The pulpit of the former Church Of The Doubting Thomas now sported a diving board (3 metre springboard variety) from which those who disagreed with Jesus were threatened with being forced to "walk the plank" to their serious injury or death. There was, after all, no water below.

I have to say that I never witnessed such an occasion.

I remember one such meeting at which I was present. Just as the weekly strategy meeting got underway, the front doorbell rang. Furious with the interruption, Jesus himself stormed down to the front church door, wrenched it open and stared at those outside with an expression on his countenance that would have reduced most human beings to a state of unmitigated terror.

"Yes?" he yelled at the elderly Dutch couple who had had the temerity to ring the doorbell.

"We wondered if we could visit the Church," an elderly Dutch woman said timorously. "We were abused here as children by the nuns and the monks and priests."

"Fuck off!" he shouted at the elderly victims of child abuse and stormed back to the former altar of The Church of The Doubting Thomas there to

roundly abuse Roberto, a Bolivian who had failed to cause the delivery of ten kilograms of cocaine to HQ Amsterdam.
"You cunt!" shouted Jesus in English at the unfortunate Bolivian.
I left at this point.
Before I leave the subject of the "Church", Jesus had, as all major organisations do, named a successor in the event of his being caught by the police of Amsterdam, Interpol and all the other organisations dedicated to the prosecution or elimination of drug smugglers and dealers. True to form he had named such an event as his "crucifixion". That successor was to be Concepcion or, as Jesus called her frequently, "the sacred feminine" upon which his "Church" was founded.
In this context it is amusing to recall that the other "disciples" often accused Jesus of not loving them as much as Concepcion!

CHAPTER SEVEN
In which Rudi, the German drug dealer describes a typical weekly business meeting.

Jesus was the type of man whom even the Spanish approve. He was a carnivore. Now, to say that there is a steakhouse on every street corner in Amsterdam is a patent exaggeration. I would say on every second street corner. (The Dutch appear to have no discernible, distinct "kitchen" unless you count coleslaw and pommes frites with everything.) Needless to say Jesus had his favourite steak houses. A curious mixture of Spanish machismo and culture, Jesus insisted that we convene our weekly management and strategy meetings (of which there were precisely two members, Jesus and myself) at an Argentinean steakhouse "round the corner" from The Hermitage, Amsterdam. (This choice had required a vote at the management and strategy committee. Travelling to this venue after all necessitated travelling there by a Number 9 tram from central Station to Waterlooplein. Tram Number two does not go to The Hermitage.)
Jesus was a wildly enthusiastic member and supporter of of a privileged group of art lovers at The Hermitage, donating some of the proceeds of his drug trafficking in return for membership of the privileged group.
At a typical business meeting Jesus usually whistled up a three hundred gram steak for himself and a two hundred gram steak for me. I watched him devour the same with quasi-medical interest. It was

akin to watching a lion or a tiger devouring raw meat and with their absolute disregard for even basic table manners. (I once suggested to Jesus that he order a vegetarian lasagne and it took all my powers of persuasion to convince him that what I had suggested was merely a jocular remark made in "poor" taste.)

Accompanying the three hundred gram steak was the usual river of Jenever and Heineken beer. Then it was down to business and the agenda for our management and strategy meeting. As always "under performing" mules topped the list of the management items on the agenda. In particular, one mule had been captured in Amsterdam and, worse, informed on us in exchange for bail pending his trial. Jesus decided that the tendons in the man's hands and arms should be slit thus reducing the man to a cripple *pour encourager les autres*. I pointed out that this was appallingly brutal. It is not, retorted Jesus. The Chinese, if annoyed, would stitch a horse hair into a man's penis. Not only would he itch for a lifetime, sexual intercourse would be an abomination. I marvelled at Chinese ingenuity in torture and expressed my admiration for his humanity in only slitting tendons. I dutifully noted the decision in the minutes for the meeting (recorded on a paper napkin belonging to the steakhouse.)

Next, we turned our attention to the items on the agenda that referred to strategy. Jesus who was a devout disciple of "the ever-expanding business" model and "never-ending race" in commerce intimated to the meeting (that is, Jesus and myself) that he favoured dealing with our Triad

competitors both here in Amsterdam and in Rotterdam. I duly noted that the proposal had been carried by two votes (that is he and I) and that there were no dissenting votes. The precise action to be taken was deferred for the consideration of our executive committee (he and I) to be held in the same steakhouse on Tuesday evening next at 8 pm.
Next, Jesus addressed the meeting on the desirability of expanding our operations in Spain. On a recent "business" trip to Madrid, he had met a Spanish woman of some consequence and standing. This encounter had occurred while floating around the dance floor of a former palacio given over to the practice of the Tango-an abiding passion in this very South American of men.
I approved of this proposal as I had already recruited two excellent Spanish mules and a Spanish speaking French girl studying in Madrid. I shall tell you more about the Spanish lady and the mules later.
A golden opportunity for expansion has arisen, Jesus concluded, and good corporate governance demanded that we avail ourselves of it. The proposal was carried unanimously and deferred for the views of the planning and strategy committee (he and I) who were to report back with recommendations by the time of the next management and strategy committee meeting to be held in the same steakhouse in precisely one week.
As secretary and in the absence of "Any Other Competent Business", I closed the meeting and signed my name at the end of my minutes and handed the same (on a paper napkin) to him. He

proposed a vote of thanks for my labours which was carried unanimously.
He then turned his attention to yet more Jenever and the Heineken.

CHAPTER EIGHT
In which Rudi, the German drug dealer, describes a musical performance given by Jesus Peron.

The early evening saw us both return to Central Station from Waterloo plein on Tram Number 9. We then took tram Number 2 and journeyed to The Concertgebouw on The Museumplein. Jesus had a musical engagement there. This engagement was not actually in The Concertgebouw where the Fifth Symphony of Mahler was being performed but outside on the street playing with his Peruvian windpipe band (now renamed "The Royal Peru Musical Ensemble" for the occasion.)

Outside most theatres, concert halls and the like round the world, "buskers" perform for waiting audiences. In some parts of the world, they are tolerated; in other parts they require permission. At The Concertgebouw, it is a bit of both. A solitary busker might be tolerated with patronising disdain but a group such as "The Royal Peru Ensemble" (as it was temporarily known) definitely required some sort of *a priori* permission which Jesus had obtained. He had somehow managed to secure a brief meeting with The Musical Director. Trading on the influence acquired as a result of his membership of the privileged group of art lovers at The Hermitage (itself the unwitting recipient of largesse from Jesus's drug trafficking profits), he succeeded in persuading The Musical Director that "The Royal Peru Ensemble" was a charitable institution which existed for the moral redemption of loose Peruvian women and had played for Heads of State in Peru and elsewhere. To that end Jesus had displayed photographs of himself and "The Ensemble" apparently receiving the warm congratulations from various Heads of State throughout the entire civilised world. (One member of the band was a dab hand at doctoring photographs on his lap-top.)

The Director of Music was so impressed that permission for the street gig was granted almost immediately. Such was the delusional psyche of Jesus' mind when it came to his own music that he instantly saw the permission as being in some way equivalent to an invitation to play in the *Grote Saal* of the Concertgebouw itself.

My duties at this performance of "The Royal Peru Ensemble" were somewhat prosaic in that all I had to do was dress up in a poncho and hat and try to sell as many copies of "The Royal Peru Ensemble" latest CD to as many spectators as I could. This I did with a conspicuous lack of success. In my humble of opinion, this was caused by the Ensemble's lack of conviction in their rendition of "Guantanamera".

CHAPTER NINE
In which Rudi, the German drug dealer, describes a typical Thursday with Jesus on his day off.

Thursdays in Amsterdam were sacrosanct. It was Jesus' day off. He liked to whore on Thursday afternoons. The whores offered half-price for Old Age Pensioners and the physically disadvantaged. (Although it was painful to watch Jesus hobble up to a whore with a stick pretending to be either disabled or over sixty-five years of age or both. My task was to wait outside and keep his wallet while he whored. "In case I get screwed" he always said (he meant had his money stolen.) In case the Russian "Gringos" came along and either assaulted him when he was least able to defend himself (that is, with his pants down) or stole his money when he was least able to prevent the robbery (that is, with his pants down.)

The Russians were, so far as he was concerned, in the same category as The Triads or The Americans. That Thursday afternoon, he studied the "menu" outside the girl's place of work in The Red Light District minutely. The "menu" as the notice affixed to the door described itself, certainly merited close study. On offer as an "hors d'oeuvre" was humiliation and degradation; as a "main course", spanking and caning and as a "desert", vaginal sex, with anal sex attracting a twenty-five euro surcharge.

Jesus mulled matters over in Spanish. I had already been given custody of his wallet and awaited the outcome of his deliberations.

In the meantime the young lady whose place of work it was came to the door to do what she could to assist Jesus in his consideration of these weighty matters. After some further moments of deep cogitation, he announced to the young lady that he had decided upon "humiliation" followed by spanking and vaginal sex, adding for good measure that anal sex was "for Arabs". The young lady to whom this was announced received Jesus' intimation of his sexual needs and requirements in the manner of a bored shop assistant receiving a grocery order.

"That will be 80 Euros, Sir," she said.

A pained expression appeared on his countenance. "Soy pobre hombre," he said in Spanish. (I am a poor man.)

The girl laughed as she toyed with the lapel of his expensive suit jacket.

"*Una Mentida*!" she exclaimed in Spanish. (A lie!)

The girl was obviously a good linguist. Now at the risk of confusing the reader, the *Lingua Franca* of The Red Light District is English and both Jesus and I were taken back by the girl's linguistic virtuosity. So much so that Jesus ordered me to give her eighty Euros from his wallet without further ado.

After tendering the young lady's fee there was nothing for me to do but stand guard outside clutching his wallet and listen to the screams coming from within. Dutch people are broadminded and even have an annual torture festival for those so inclined. That said (and I suppose it must be my sheltered upbringing), I do find it a touch extreme standing outside a whore's place of work in Amsterdam listening to my employer (even if he was a major drug smuggler) being soundly beaten. Although I must confess there was a certain satisfaction in listening to him being roundly abused. The surreal aspect of this occasion was heightened by a party of Dutch schoolchildren passing by just as the young lady got into her stride in her application of the full weight of her hand to his posterior.

Eventually, the young lady (who had clearly warmed to her task during the performance thereof) concluded her labours and Jesus ceased to scream. At last he appeared at the door and seizing his wallet from my hand, withdrew a 20 Euro Note from the aforesaid wallet and passed it to the young lady as a "bonus" for "good work".

He was always tired and depressed after his whoring on Thursday afternoons. On one such occasion I suggested that he take some of the cocaine he smuggled in such vast quantities to improve his mood.

He looked at me as if I were mad and taken complete leave of my senses. As I have said, he was clean when it came to drugs (excluding alcohol, that is.)

"God knew," he pronounced solemnly, "that his finest creation would become tired from time to time," said Jesus with religious solemnity. "That is why God made Red Bull."

I knew better than to offer any comment. Jesus survived on 16 Red Bulls a day and endless painkillers.

Thursday evenings were usually spent at a classical concert or recital-if there was one to be had which met with his exacting musical standards.

The routine was almost invariable. We would board the Number Two Tram into town and get off near The Concertgebouw. From there it was back across the road and into one of his favourite eateries called "The Small Talk" a short few metres from the concert hall. There he would whistle up Jenevers and large Heineken beers. These were provided to him by a corpulent barman with whom he was friendly by dint of countless attendances in the aforesaid establishment.

The middle-class clientele were, in my view, always tolerant of a man in their midst who resembled Che Guevara right down to the cigar he smoked in the premises without complaint from anyone.

Then it would be off to the concert.

Concert or recital over, Jesus invariably announced that he was "thirsty" and accordingly we repaired to premises just across the road from The Concertgebouw called the Keyser. It was a restaurant at lunchtime and for the hours of dinner in the evening. At other hours of the day it functioned as a cafe/bistro/bar. Jesus never had difficulty in securing a table. I remember one amusing occasion when a darkly good-looking waitress attended upon us at the table we had taken. She was an Amsterdamer of mixed race and Jesus eyed her shamelessly, libidinously and

lasciviously. He had no rules about having carnal relations with any girl so long as she was not one of his mules.
"Eres Bonita, Senorita," Jesus.
The girl understood. Whether she had any command of the Spanish tongue, I do not know. In any event, his meaning (and intentions) was abundantly obvious. The girl was not incommoded. No doubt she was well accustomed to her pulchritude being openly admired.
"What would you like to drink, Sir?"
"Drink?" Jesus. "Why would anyone want to drink with such a beautiful young woman to woo?"
The girl began to lose patience.
"What would you like to drink, Sir?" she repeated and this time coldly.
Jesus took the hint, gave up (for once) and ordered that a river of Jenever and Heineken descend upon us.
Thus did his typical day off on a Thursday draw to a conclusion.

CHAPTER TEN
In which Rudi, the German drug dealer, further describes his duties in Germany.

Among my myriad duties as Jesus' lieutenant and factotum was one task of which I was very fond: that of manager and sole crew member of his powerful motor cruiser called "The Shining Path" after some revolutionary outfit in South America (Peru I think).
Jesus had purchased this beast of a vehicle after a particularly successful operation which had netted him over 32 million Euros in one fell swoop. "The Shining Path" was moored on the Rhine near Cologne and Jesus was wont to repair there whenever his soul was troubled (a not infrequent occurrence).
As regards the purchase of the boat, it is difficult for a highly successful drug trafficker to know what to do with all the money without arousing suspicion. In my humble experience, one can soon run out of safe havens and money laundering devices of which Jesus' "coffee-shop" next to the Royal palace in Amsterdam was quite the most breathtakingly brazen. He often remarked that he purchased the boat in order to provide back-up for mules if they got into difficulties but I think he really purchased it for pleasure.
On Sundays and if the weather was good, I would receive a phone call not much after seven am intimating that we should be aboard "The Shining

Path" by nine am. It is quite impossible to drive from Amsterdam to the boat's mooring south of Cologne in that time but Jesus always summoned his chopper.

From Cologne he would direct me to pilot the boat south to Koblenz and the Deutches Eck (The German Corner) which commanded the confluence of the rivers Rhine and Mosel (or Moselle if you are English).

I knew why Jesus liked that place and I will explain. *Machismo* is not, in my opinion, an attractive characteristic implying, as it does, that the person who possesses it is "manly", "big-hearted" and disposed to grandiloquence and dramatic and theatrical displays designed to emphasise such supposed virtues. It is, in short, for men and women of low intelligence-people who adore War Movies and Westerns. Now, as I have said, Jesus was highly intelligent but this did not preclude a propensity for *machismo*, a consequence of his cultural background no doubt.

The "German Corner" for him was a statement of German Machismo, if there be such a thing. A crass, monstrous monument in blackened stone with a towering equestrian statue of Kaiser Wilhelm the First greets the visitor at the confluence of the two rivers with a large German flag atop fluttering in the breeze. Jesus wildly approved of the monstrosity and would sit back in the white leather seats of the motor cruiser sipping some Peruvian alcoholic concoction guaranteed to separate the imbiber from several thousand brain cells with every glass.

I always enjoyed our trips down (or is it up?) the Rhine. There was one very good reason for my enjoyment: I had been born and brought up in the Rhineland town of Rudesheim. Now of course every nation suffers from inter-regional prejudices which are awash with stereotypes and Germany is no exception. Thus do the Berliners scorn the Bavarians (and vice-versa) and even educated Germans can, of occasion, barely resist a libellous swipe at the Rhinelander who is stereotypically considered to be fat, lazy and sodden in wine. While aware of such matters, nothing could spoil my excursions with Jesus to an area which I still considered to be my home.

Further, in the same way as our criminal enterprises in Amsterdam were concentrated on the artery that was the route of tram number two, I made the Rhine River a vital artery in our business. The Rhine has always been a major artery of trade throughout the centuries and (rightly) in my opinion is considered to be one of the world's greatest rivers. I ran the operations in the area under his supervision. My contribution to the river's legendary reputation as a trade artery was to turn it into the main artery for our illicit drug smuggling in Europe. The smuggling routes ran through The Czech Republic, Slovakia, Romania, Hungary, Austria, Switzerland and Lichtenstein which even Jesus regarded as a den of iniquity. Prior to the arrival of the mules on German soil, Jesus was always in a paroxysm of anxiety lest they be detected.

Upon arrival on German soil, a mule travelled upriver (or is it down river? I must enquire of a reputable geographer what the answer is to this vexed question) to Koblenz where there is a hub railway station. This they did by a variety of methods ranging from pleasure craft to road (or on one occasion, somewhat memorably, by bicycle!) Once on the train from Koblenz it was plain sailing, if I may be forgiven the mixed metaphor. Jesus adored German railways and once regaled me with what he had discovered in a history book, namely that at the outbreak of The First World War, the Germany army had moved three and a half million men by train. Three and a half million men by railway! He repeated for emphasis. (It was unwise of me to enquire if he intended to move three and a half million mules by the same mode of transport.)

The mules arrived in Cologne and from there the drugs were despatched by a variety of means to the centre of our operations, namely Amsterdam.

CHAPTER ELEVEN
In which Rudi, the German drug dealer, describes Norma the mule.

This is an appropriate place in my statement to give a description of the mule that was to prove the downfall of us all. Her name was Norma and I hated her from the first moment I saw her. Appropriately enough Jesus and I met her on Tram Number Two. We were on our way to a concert at the Concertgebouw and so was she. I can't remember how the conversation started on the tram. If memory serves, the tram jolted suddenly and she fell against Jesus. He made a joke about the incident and it all developed from that.
She was twenty-six years of age, startlingly attractive and the daughter of a well-to-do lawyer whose nationality escapes me. She was five foot seven inches in height, sixty five kilograms, of mixed race and usually wore jeans and a black leather jacket.
Ah, the flotsam and slagheap of humanity to be found in the world of drug addiction and drug smuggling! That said some had been worthwhile human beings prior to their fall from grace. Take Jesus, he should have been a great doctor. Take me; I should have been a concert violinist, pianist or guitarist. What became of us? We were both now drug pedlars, Jesus played in a Peruvian wind band and I played in any musical ensemble that would have me.
Now what should the mule Norma have been? She was a spoiled brat so typical of the grand

bourgeoisie anywhere in the world. Her parents had brought her up to believe that she was the beautiful daughter of the privileged classes. The result was that she was utterly contemptuous of other people's rights and feelings and was herself contemptible. The poor little rich girl had read law and obtained a degree. She had then cast her eyes around this world and wondered why she should have to work for a living at all. Why indeed? What with indulgent parents and grandparents, she wanted for nothing. After a brief spell in Post Office management (One does have to wonder why-given the legal tradition of her family) she quit her job after fellow employees failed to accord her the "respect" she thought she was entitled to. Next she squandered her allowance. Profligate, lacking in self-discipline and totally without what they call a "moral compass" these days, she abandoned herself to all manner of sexual depravity, said course of conduct leading to her contracting venereal disease. Her endlessly indulgent family put a brave face on matters, declaring to all who would listen that such things happen "in the best regulated of circles". They do not.
Eventually even her indulgent parents wearied of this appalling shrew.
And after all that, guess what? After she had literally banged into Jesus, The Big Boss Man of The Whole Scene decided that he liked this fallen woman. I can make use of this worthless whore, he opined and recruited her as a mule. Now Jesus had an inviolable rule: he never recruited a mule who was an addict and that for the very obvious reason that they were so unreliable. Worthless whore as

she was, she only used drugs recreationally. She never snorted on the job, if you take my meaning. Jesus and I disagreed violently over the employment of the mule whore Norma. Jesus pointed out that she was well-connected what with being the daughter of a well-known lawyer and could therefore move with ease in the best of circles and was therefore an asset to us. I countered this by arguing that this was exactly made her a danger for our organisation. She was a wilful, spoiled brat, a poor little rich girl who would not hesitate to betray us if her own skin was in danger. I have to confess that I like my girls to be poor or, if they are rich, to have made their own money. Not some brainless brat who is dependent on "Daddy" for economic salvation. That kind of brat comes into this world and perceives that "Daddy" has money, everything that brings with it and that "Daddy" has status and influence in life which the poor little rich brat is determined to maintain on her own account. Her "Mummy" is some poor fish who married "Daddy" and basks in the reflected glory of Daddy.

The fun really starts in the poor little rich girl's life in two circumstances: when she has to start work and when she meets a man she really wants. In the case of work, the poor little rich girl does not see why she should slave away like fuck for money when Daddy has so much of the fucking stuff and is tempted to take shortcuts for example steal the stuff or marry some rich prick who can keep her in the style to which she is accustomed, as they say. This brings me neatly to the next point in the poor little rich girl's life where the fun really starts or rather all hell breaks loose. Firstly after the brat has experienced the "sexual awakening" as our ghastly friends in psychology call it, she sleeps with anything that comes along from the local dustman to the local Man of God. The action really starts when the poor little rich brat spots someone whom she really wants. Then, suddenly, it is as if she had never behaved like a street whore. All manner of criteria are applied to the consideration of the object of her interest which was never applied to the local dustman or the local Man of God. Any woman, even a poor little rich brat, is innately subservient to the wishes of her parents and class peers, especially when it comes to the choice of a potential life-long mate. Thus the object of her interest must meet with the approval of her Papa, her Mama and the poor little rich brat's peers. In the very nature of life fault will be found with the object of her interest. Perhaps his eyebrows are two bushy or he has been known to scratch his posterior in public or, more seriously, did not attend "the right school" or university, does not golf at the best of clubs, does not have enough money or is a mere accountant rather than being a star of the diplomatic service and titled. Add to all that the poor little rich brat has to come to terms with her own emotions. Meeting someone she might like causes many turbulent emotions, none worse than the fact it means she will have children by that man. That is worse than having her legs waxed after all.

Before the poor little rich brat knows where she is she has allowed herself to be persuaded (and sometimes by envious, malicious girlfriends) that

the object of her interest is not, after all, the "love of her life". She loses all interest sometimes with the consequence of life-long regret.
That is why I hate and deeply distrust poor little rich brats and vastly prefer the poor such as the divine Concepcion. At least she was independent and could take her own decisions without reference to "Daddy", "Mummy" or her peers. The rich are always trouble and so it proved with Norma the mule whore.
It was Norma the mule whore who shopped all of us to the police and right in the middle of the Barcelona business. I shall shortly describe the Barcelona business in some detail.

Norma the mule whore was what I would call a "category one" mule. Let me explain what I mean. There is, as some of you may be aware, a certain hierarchy for mules. There are the poor bastards who have the most dangerous task of all-taking delivery of a consignment once it has landed in a country and then taking it to the point of distribution. I describe these mules as "category one" mules. Assuming the mule gets through, the most urgent task is to distribute the drugs as quickly as possible and for very obvious reasons. In the case of a consignment relating to our Amsterdam operations it was part of my job to meet the mule, check the consignment was correct, pay the mule and send him (or her) on his (or her) way with dire threats as to the consequences for their health should they breathe a word of the transaction.

Let me illustrate this procedure by reference to a typical transaction with Norma the Mule.

On a morning in May a few days before she shopped us all, I was ensconced in the Cafe des Amis at my favourite table (facing the police station) and, as they say in the musical "South Pacific", whistling, or in my case, humming, a happy tune. As it was springtime in Amsterdam, I had selected "Tulips from Amsterdam" to hum. (It had occurred to me to rename the song "Cocaine from Amsterdam" but that would have been unforgivably dashing and Cavalier, given the circumstances.)

I was alone. Jesus, who normally would have been in attendance for the delivery of such an important consignment, had a street gig in town. I never ceased to marvel at his God-like detachment from reality and his apparent lack of any sense of priority. Do not misunderstand me, he was no coke head. He was clean. It was just that he valued his Peruvian music above all else with the possible exception of dancing the Tango.

Norma the Mule arrived. I watched as she left the Number two tram and then made for the Cafe des Amis with neither a glance to her left or right. That was good. She seemed to know exactly what she was about. (I had had the misfortune to work with mules who looked suspicious at first glance when delivering a consignment.) Norma the Mule was reassuringly confident.

Her eyes swept the interior of the Cafe des Amis. There was little to register. It was ten past eleven on that May Tuesday morning. Apart from my good self, apparently absorbed in consuming his double espresso, there were only two Dutch ladies of indeterminate age and two young mothers with fractious children enjoying the ambience and service of the Cafe des Amis.

I am naturally a cautious man and prior to engaging with her in the absurd charade we used on such occasions for us by way of ascertaining that she had not been tailed and all had gone well, I cast a wary eye over the nearby police station and what I could see of its occupants. Nothing I could discern caused me apprehension. I got up and made for the door, pausing at the table she had selected.

"I find it impossible to stop smoking."

"So do I."

"Perhaps you will join me?"

"My mother advised me never to consort with strange men."

"Even so."

Charade over, she got up and accompanied me to the door of the Cafe des Amis, bringing her weighty rucksack with her.

 "Did you have any trouble on the way in from Zeeland?" (Zeeland is in South West of the Netherlands.) Our cartel's high speed power boats landed the consignments there and whores (I mean mules, the likes of Norma) picked them up and delivered them to Amsterdam.

"No, no trouble," she replied as she drew on the cigarette I had given her and lit for her.

She did not have a lot going for her, I reflected. Estranged from her family and suffering from venereal disease, it was quite unnecessary for me to recall the strict rule for people like me who interact with mules namely that carnal relations were strictly forbidden. This policy was based on the premise that sexual relations between one of his trusted lieutenants and a mere mule would inevitably lead to divided loyalties. Jesus need not have worried. The mere idea of sex with "The Carrier Bag" as she was known would have made me ill.

After I parted company with her, I went over to Jesus' pad across the road and dumped the high value consignment of cocaine there.

CHAPTER TWELVE
In which Rudi, the German drug dealer, describes some of the dangers in drug smuggling; a "star" mule in Barcelona; Maria de G..., a Madrid woman Jesus had fallen for and the three mules Rudi had himself recruited.

In the life of an international drug smuggler there are critical points at which the danger is heightened and the accompanying tension palpable.
Firstly there is the point of departure of the consignment and the larger the consignment the greater the danger. Every country nowadays—for good or for ill—has a variety of agencies combating "the drug menace" and in addition alongside the police and customs forces and drug squads are the liaison officers of other countries. All work for the common good and with common objectives. That at least is the theory. In practice, they vie with each other to secure the kudos from government which the netting of a large drugs haul brings. After all it is commensurately easier for an agency to obtain government funding in the wake of seizing a large haul.
Secondly the point of entry into a country is also fraught with dangers. Various methods of bringing drugs "ashore" are well known, for example the cargo ships that sail the world's waterways off-loading to powerful speed boats or the use of

container ports. If a land border must be crossed the use of large heavy goods vehicles is scarcely unknown.

Jesus Maria Magdalena Peron was quite prepared to use any or all of these methods. One method of bringing drugs into a country was truly breathtaking. Early on in his international "career" as a drug smuggler he hit on this staggering solution. He noticed that there was one type of man or woman who travelled the world of narcotics unchallenged and they were the liaison officers. Quite legitimately they could be in any South American country one day and turn up anywhere in Europe the next. His "star" courier or mule was therefore an American naval officer whose primary duties were that of a liaison officer. He was subject only to the most cursory of examination by customs and passport people and, in any event, usually travelled by military planes where inspection of his possessions were non-existent given his high security clearance.

The third danger point is that even where the dangers of the point of departure and the point of entry have been successfully negotiated, the consignment must be "cut" into smaller deals and distributed to lesser dealers as swiftly as possible. At this stage people who cannot necessarily be trusted are involved. Tongues wag or the distribution network may have been infiltrated. Only when the consignment has been cut and distributed can the drug smuggler to some extent relax.

Jesus received word that the American naval officer was about to bring in twenty-five kilograms of the

purest cocaine into Barcelona. I can safely say that I never saw Jesus more animated. He decided that one of my mules based in Barcelona would meet the officer in the middle of that well known street for tourists The Ramblas. Her name was Consuela M.... She would then convey the twenty-five kilograms to Gaudi's Sagrada Familia where the consignment would be transferred into the custody of another of my mules who would take it to Madrid. (Jesus was a great believer in using multiple trusted couriers on the basis that one mule was easily identified and followed.) Her name was Vanessa S.... In Madrid he would have one of his most trusted associates meet her and together with my third mule, Agnes Le B... who came from Versailles outside Paris they would convey the consignment to Versailles where the usual Amsterdam couriers would take over.
Before I describe this operation in greater detail it seems appropriate to give some description of the "dramatis personae", that is the mules and especially those whom I recruited.

However let me first tell you about a mule whom Jesus personally recruited.
Jesus was fussy about the women he allowed in his life. They had "to count" as he put it. One such woman was the grand-daughter of one of Franco's generals. She was older than he was. This woman bore the name Maria de G.... Jesus had met her in a former palacio in Madrid and which now served as an upmarket dance club for aficionados of the Tango. Jesus was a master of the dance.

Maria was one of those grandees of Spanish society and not because of her father's military background. Her mother had bequeathed her one of the more desirable estates near Toledo. She was no parvenu (unlike her father, a social and military arriviste if ever there was one.) She was a woman who was born to rule and as I had become one of Jesus' most trusted lieutenants he decided that I should meet his other most trusted lieutenant.
I was sent to Madrid before journeying on to Barcelona.
As instructed by Jesus I meant her in the foyer of The Ritz Hotel in Madrid on the Paseo Prado. She was everything Jesus had led me to believe she was. Now the foyer of The Ritz was, in those days, a bit like a large conservatory. By that I mean there were many large green plants therein. I suppose the intention of management was that the guests should be soothed by a green ambience. It was mid afternoon and there were few people around save some vulgar Americans who, horror of horrors, were wearing jeans. I found Maria sitting in near proximity to where a young lady was melodiously offering renditions of classical pieces on the harp. (The Ritz in Madrid does not do vulgar bar pianists.)
I had only just set eyes on her when I almost instantly realised why Jesus valued her so. I estimated that she was in her mid-forties. Maria de G... had what the Spanish would indelicately call a full figure but with no trace of obesity. Even given middle-age she still had a full head of very black hair. The eyes were a deep brown-or at least so I saw when, as a matter of courtesy, she removed her

sun glasses. Her clothes were predominantly black in colour and severely cut to my inexpert eye but somehow managing an exquisite balance between sartorial elegance with something of a concession to her undoubted femininity without a trace of vulgarity. I was bidden to sit down and she made enquiry as to what I wished to drink. (I noticed that she herself had contented herself with what appeared to be a humble cortado.) Had I not been so intimidated by her self-assured manner, I doubtless would have contented myself with the same. Her manner however overcame my natural caution and I requested a cognac. A waiter appeared almost without summons. A bottle of rare Courvoisier appeared and a modicum of a measure was poured.

The lady's self containment was something to behold. She intimated that she had little time to spare and indicated that her driver (a swarthy gentleman standing by the entrance who divided his attention between scrutiny of me and her orange Aston Martin just visible beyond the entrance) was expecting to imminently convey her urgently to a destination which Maria de G... did not find necessary to disclose to me.

She ran over the brief details of the current operation with apologies for her reference thereto as she presumed I was entirely conversant with the detail.

Meeting with the other most trusted lieutenant of Jesus over, it was off to Barcelona to rendezvous with the man himself.

Now I shall provide a brief description of the three mules I had recruited beginning with Consuela S...

in Barcelona. She was instructed to meet the American naval and liaison officer.

I first visited the city of Barcelona many years ago travelling there by a budget airline. On the flight I got talking to an American girl. She told me that she was the daughter of an American Marine Officer. Now I don't like soldiers or anything military but a girl is a girl. Her name was Consuela M... and she was very attractive, spoke beautiful Spanish and had travelled round all the South American countries. The establishment in Britain and the United States hate these countries. They are regarded as being Communist at heart. (Anyone in the world who can speak a foreign language is, according to the Americans, a Communist bastard, especially them thar Spanish speaking sons-of-bitches.)

We got on great and shared a taxi into downtown Barcelona. She gave the taxi-driver his marching orders explaining that "El Senor" (she meant me) was staying at a hotel smack in the middle of "Las Ramblas". My Spanish in those days was practically non-existent and I said nothing. The taxi driver did not like me. I could tell by the way he looked at me in his rear-view mirror. He was obviously suspicious of a non-Spanish speaking prick shagging some beautiful Spanish-speaking girl. I wanted to tell him that she was only an American Marine's daughter and he shouldn't complain but I didn't know the Spanish for that.

Anyway I didn't expect to see Ms American Marine Officer's daughter again after she instructed the taxi-driver to drop me off at my downtown hotel in Barcelona. But I must have made a better

impression on her than I thought! Next day after a shower and a shave there was a phone call from the foyer. EL Senor? Yeah, that's me. (I was getting used to being called "El Senor".) There's a girl down here to see you.
OK, OK, I'll be down right away. Well, wouldn't you do the same? Now Barcelona is a port at which detachments of the American Sixth Fleet calls so I was careful when I went down to the foyer. There could have been a detachment of marines down there after all. But no it was just her.
I was just passing she said and I thought about you being here. Fair enough, said I. I've just been for a blood test, she said. (Apparently the Spanish want a blood test for AIDS if you apply for a job.) OK, said I. Lunch? Sure, thought you'd never ask, she replied.
She knew the place (Barcelona, I mean) and took me off to a Bistro in downtown Barcelona.
It went well. In the course of the meal I remember she introduced me to the Spanish word for puddings or desserts which I did not know. Los Postres. I have never forgotten that Spanish word. To finish lunch, she asked me to order two brandies. Lepantos! The girl knew her brandies! A girl who whistles up a couple of brandies with a man she hardly knows has made a decision!
We went back to my hotel and made love.
Consuela was married but unhappily so. I had an affair with her. You could say that it was something of a whirlwind romance. I told her that I was a classically trained musician and also worked for a company in Amsterdam which sold medicinal products. Early on in the relationship I told her

that I used drugs recreationally. This is not illegal in Spain provided they are for personal use. Given the heady romance of our relationship in those early days it was not difficult to persuade her to deliver "packages" to my friends in Barcelona when it was not expedient for me so to do. She no doubt suspected what substances were in the packages but I never provided any details. In that way and by those means she became a mule

My second mule was undoubtedly my favourite. She was a Madrilène, a waitress in the Cafe des Amis and her husband, who was a policeman, occasionally worked in the station just across from road. Her name was Vanessa S... and I got on very well with her from the start. She was an open, vivacious girl from Madrid (unlike the mule whore Norma), she did not have venereal disease and she went about her duties with zest. She was also the right colour scheme for me. She had jet-black hair and brown-almost black eyes.
We were accustomed to kissing each other three times on the cheek when we met (following the Dutch custom.) One morning, when the Cafe des Amis had little custom and we had exchanged greetings in the customary manner, she intimated to me that the zip of her skirt was giving her trouble and would I possibly try to rectify the matter? Of course, I replied-ever the Gentleman. Best that you try to deal with the troublesome zip in the staff loo she advised. Otherwise the solitary customer of The Cafe des Amis that morning might think that we are on terms of intimacy. Of course, replied I, the Gentleman. I was completely sober and of sane

senses that morning but for the life of me I cannot recall in the blur of breathtaking intimacy that followed in the staff loo whether Vanessa shagged me or I shagged her. I am clear however that intimacy occurred. In the weeks that followed, intimacy occurred in cars, hotel beds and occasionally in the staff loo of the Cafe des Amis—the scene of the original crime.

I decided to recruit her. Vanessa was 34 years old and her husband, the policeman, was 33. They were hard up what with the shocking cost of housing in Amsterdam and day-to-day living expenses. Only drug suppliers such as me can afford to live in Amsterdam.

"Two thousand Euros for every delivery you make to Rotterdam," I announced after she had taken no exception to her recruitment. (I was paying over the going rate but I decided that she was entitled to a bonus in respect of her personal services to me.) Now I can almost hear my readers mouthing objections to this narration of events. You said that Jesus did not permit carnal relations between his trusted lieutenant and a mule. That is correct but I had had carnal relations with her prior to recruiting her. Further, I can hear my readers say, taking cocaine to Rotterdam is rather like taking coals to Newcastle. That is also correct but there are always "turf wars" between drug suppliers. For completeness I have to add that I am sure Vanessa's husband knew about me. I rather think he just endured matters. After all I paid his wife good money. Vanessa did not seem to worry about the matter. I could never decide whether she loved me or, to employ modern parlance, saw me as a "fuck buddy".

As I have said, Jesus liked his girls to be Spanish or, at least, Spanish speaking (which failing, Italian as a poor second).
The next mule I recruited on my own account Agnes was neither Spanish nor even Italian. She was French but had the saving grace of being Spanish speaking and studying in Madrid at the time I met her. Jesus therefore reluctantly sanctioned her recruitment.
We met in the most alarming of circumstances. We bumped into each other at the Queen Sophia Museum and Art gallery on a morning in Madrid in front of Picasso's Guernica. The place had just opened. We were admiring Picasso's over large graffiti (my disrespectful opinion of The Guernica) when two men in uniform came tearing along the corridor frantically fixing their ties. The Spanish guard The Guernica with two men on permanent guard duty (or did so in those days.) The guards were late for work, hence their urgency. Within moments they were either side of The Guernica and eying Agnes and I with a good deal of suspicion.
We concluded our inspection of the large graffiti and I suggested to Agnes that perhaps we should join forces for the day. She already knew (and it required no guesswork) that I was a tourist. I intended to visit The Royal Palace next. Would she like to come with? She consented.
Agnes did not like the Royal palace in Madrid and intimated that she favoured the attentions of

Madame Guillotine for the royalty of any country. I should here explain that Agnes came from Versailles and was therefore traditional in her views of what should become of Royalty. She was almost the same age as myself and I found myself very attracted to her. She studied veterinary science at the eponymous, prestigious Madrid school and lived during term time in some barrio or other in the city. The flat next door to hers was occupied by a Spanish couple who, according to Agnes, conducted themselves in the traditional Spanish manner-that is to say that they fought like cat and dog and made an intolerable din heaping imprecations on each other in the worst the Spanish tongue can summon to a human being's lips.

After The Royal Visit (for want of a better description) we wandered into The Plaza Catalunya where my hotel was. In the foyer I had a beer and Agnes a soft drink (she was teetotal).

During the ensuing conversation, questions arose as to the places of interest I should visit next. I explained that I would have to consult my tourist book. Where is it? She asked. I replied that it was in my room. We can always go and get it, said Agnes. My regard for teetotal French girls rose to new heights.

When I told Jesus about this girl and my plans to recruit her, he, with his love of Argentinean steaks, somehow managed to draw some sort of obscure parallel between her study of veterinary science and his consumption of fine cuts of meat and waxed eloquently about my choice of a new mule.

I invited her to Amsterdam. In the course of her stay there I told her that I dabbled in soft drugs and procured the same for my own personal use and occasionally for my friends. I asked her if she would deliver a package to a business acquaintance in Madrid containing a small quantity of soft drugs. Eventually she agreed to do so. This was trial run, a test to see if she could be trusted. The package contained only chocolates. She passed this test with the proverbial flying colours and was then recruited.
It was only after I had recruited her that it emerged that she knew Maria d... G... having done field work at the latter's estate outside Toledo.

As I have said the size of the American officer's consignment due for delivery to Barcelona required the attendance of Jesus himself and me to superintend matters.
It will come as no surprise to the lawyers (and, perish the thought, those most intellectually challenged of God's creation, policemen) that a larger than life creature such as Jesus, adored Barcelona. It was the city of Gaudi, the Catalans and, of course The Sagrada Familia. Of course he adored the place and had even invested in a Gaudi apartment.
The night before the delivery of the consignment by the American officer Jesus decided that he and I should attend a performance in The Opera House. There never was a Royal box in the Gran Teatre Del Liceu on the very sensible basis that the then Spanish Queen did not contribute to the Liceu's construction and therefore why should anyone give

her a Royal box? And the rest of the boxes were got rid of in the reconstruction that followed the fire of 1994. That said, Jesus bought the most expensive seats he could. The performance on that night in 2013 was Kurt Weill's "Street Scene" which in my humble opinion hardly qualified as opera in the traditional sense.

Prior to our attendance in The Opera House, Jesus, as was his wont, had insisted on my attendance in The Hard Rock Cafe on The Plaza Catalunya at the top of Las Ramblas there for me to watch him devour a three hundred gram steak. Not content with that, Jesus next conducted me to a Tapas place on Las Ramblas there to devour whatever took his interest. And then it was to the opera house.

It was during the interval at the opera that Jesus announced that his plans for a large expansion of business in Spain would be going ahead.

Prior to his recruitment of the American naval officer, Jesus imported many of his drug consignments through Galicia, a province in the north of Spain, or as Jesus referred to it in Spanish, "El Norte". They arrived in the transatlantic ships and were then downloaded to the fast speedboats and landed on deserted Galician coasts. What Jesus planned was a vast expansion of the trade by using the unwitting assistance of The American navy and its officers. (They are greedy bastards he opined. They all want to buy a house in Washington but the greedy Gringos cannot afford it unless they take my drug money.)

Up until this point the Spanish operations had consisted of Consuela M... gathering together the consignments of the mules working between

Morocco, Malaga and the Costa del Sol together with any consignments landed in Barcelona itself and then conveying them to Sagrada Familia and the clutches of Vanessa S.... Thereafter the entire haul was taken to Madrid for delivery to Agnes Le B... and Maria de G...
Under the latter's supervision all consignments would be conveyed to Versailles where the Amsterdam network would take over.

The following morning after the visit to the Opera House and once we had had breakfast, we headed for the Plaza Mayor not far from the Ramblas, there for Jesus to superintend the handover of the American officer's consignment to Consuela M....
We took seats outside a cafe in the Square. Jesus ordered brandies and coffee. It was almost midday and the flea market in the Square was beginning to attract custom from locals and tourists alike.
We did not have long to wait. The American naval officer entered the Square and made to approach Consuela. For those of my readers who have never visited Barcelona this excited no interest whatsoever. The city is a port and while the home base for the American Sixth Fleet is Naples, visits to Barcelona by the fleet's ships and personnel are hardly unknown. And Consuela was seen as just another girl plying her trade, an impression reinforced by her short leather skirt and near transparent blouse. The couple departed in the direction of the Ramblas.
Jesus summoned a waiter, paid our bill and sometime later it was off to Sagrada Familia to watch the next handover.

Jesus always had nightmares about using the Sagrada Familia in his chain of pick-up points. "Dios Mios!" he would often exclaim in Spanish when the subject came up and "May God forgive me!" in English were frequent utterances.
In the event and despite the palpable tension we both felt as we watched the handover to Vanessa S...and her husband, it went smoothly. With great relief we watched both set off in a large, hired campervan for Madrid. (They needed a large campervan. There was twenty-five kilograms of the damned stuff.)

Before ending my narration of Spanish operations so far as be known to me I should add that Jesus did not confine his activities to Madrid or Barcelona. Even the Costas took his attention if only because many of his mules passed through them on the way back from Morocco.
Castillo de Sohail, Fuengirola was one of those places on the Costas where the Spanish remind themselves that they are Spanish and not a minority ethnic group living under the rule of the moronic tourist hordes from Northern Europe who spend their time pickled in alcohol.
Castillo de Sohail, Fuengirola has an old fort with the Spanish flag fluttering atop the battlements. It was as if to say that the Costa del Sol was still sovereign Spain and that the writ of Spanish law still ran in Fuengirola.
Jesus adored the place. God knows why. I think that he concluded that he was less likely to be the subject of surveillance by the Spanish authorities in The Costas. After all, the authorities would reason

that no civilised man would maintain a residence in such benighted places.

He maintained a magnificent residence outside Fuengirola on a rock promontory with a commanding view of the town, the bay and the Mediterranean. Paradoxically, for a "devout" communist, he had named the villa "Castillo Del Rey" and from there he superintended much of his Spanish drug trafficking operations. Jesus was truly an outrageous man.

It will come as no surprise to my readers that Jesus was well versed in Spanish law: he had to be when things occasionally went wrong. Jesus could have made it to the top of the Spanish legal profession or anyone's legal profession. He was, as he put it colourfully himself, "shit hot" in Spanish law. So why had he not become an abogado instead of a drug trafficker, I asked? He called me an Estupido. Did I not know that all lawyers were crooks?

He was very keen on Spanish universal criminal jurisdiction for George Bush and Tony Blair but not for his own "minor" pecadillos in international "pharmacy" as he put it.

CHAPTER THIRTEEN
In which Rudi, the German drug dealer describes how Norma the mule's love of diamonds wrecked the entire organisation

Before I proceed with a narration of the appalling trouble she caused us, I want to say something about diamonds, a subject which I knew very little about until recent times.
Diamonds are of course, in the words of the old song, a girl's best friend of course. Small in comparison to gold bars, I am sure you would agree and ideal for smuggling. I once saw an uncut blue in a diamond cutters place of business in Amsterdam said to be worth a cool $6 million once cut and polished. It didn't look much to my untutored eye. (By the by, it has always amused me that most girlies think all diamonds are white and clear. De Beers have, or used to have, a fabulous collection of "Fancies" as the coloured diamonds are known.)
Well, on with the tale of woe that Norma the mule whore got into and how she wrecked the organisation.
One day in early May I was sitting on Tram Number Two when my Moby went off. It was her. The police at Schipol airport had allowed her to make the call. She had been caught with a huge uncut blue. She really was a stupid bitch. Why call me? I hung up immediately and phoned Jesus. My Spanish was not good enough to translate the

torrent of abuse that came down into my phone. I was horribly tempted to say "I told you so" but refrained. I wanted to live a little longer.
Poor little rich brats are always trouble.
The story of how she came to be caught with a huge uncut blue is as follows.
The poor little spoiled disgraced whore had had a "peach" of an idea to make money and repair her finances. (I thought Jesus was paying her enough as it was.) She decided to pop down to Jo'burg first class by KLM and bring back whatever she could. On her return an alert customs man had decided to have a rummage in her soiled knickers and there was the monster uncut blue.
There was no defence. So Daddy, being a lawyer, phoned one of his pals, The President of The United States (another lawyer-why do Americans always have lawyers as Presidents-too many war crimes?) and pleaded with him. Daughter was just a headstrong girl who had experienced a moment of madness and could the good offices of The President be put to the purpose of getting her off? Meanwhile Jesus was, as they, incandescent with rage. (In his case, almost literally, and threatened to cut her nipples off if she breathed a word about our honest-to-goodness drug trafficking business.) When Concepcion learned of what had happened she agreed with me that spoiled little rich brats are trouble.
As those who read this statement well know, Norma the mule whore spilled the beans in order to try and save her own rotten skin and the arrests began.

CHAPTER FOURTEEN
Extract of a statement given to the police of Amsterdam on 1 May 2013 by Concepcion d...l...C....

My full name is Concepcion d...l...C... and I am 23 years of age having been born in the district of Steglitz Berlin on 22 April 1990.
My parents are citizens of Peru and of peasant stock. In 1990 they travelled to Berlin as part of an extended family group seeking a new life there. They had wearied of the perennial cycles of repression by landowners and governments. It is relevant to establish at the very outset of this statement that the descendents of South American Indians have their own vibrant and ancient culture a small part of which does include what the West terms narcotics. Such people as my parents see nothing wrong with the uses-in all its forms-of the cocoa plant both as a means of scratching a living and as a necessary means of escape from the harsh vicissitudes and cruel vagaries of life. It is bewildering for them to learn of western governments' much publicised prouncements on "the war against drugs". The international law definition of war is a state of hostilities between sovereign nations. It is not a word to be bandied about by cheapskate politicians or stupid policemen. As has been noted by international studies on the subject of drugs the biggest drug pedlars in the world are governments particularly those of the United States of America and the United Kingdom (as it likes to call itself).

Even a cursory examination of history by an unskilled historian supports that proposition. It is necessary to cite but a few examples: the British, when their Empire was at its zenith, fought the opium wars with China and catapulted millions of Chinese into addiction; the use of drugs by the United States government to cause addiction and destabilisation and to provide funding for and in their "dirty" wars in the countries of South America; the use of drugs for similar purposes in Laos, Cambodia and Vietnam and in the Middle East the use of drugs and arms for hostages. (This appalling trade reached new depths when a 747 Jumbo Jet was brought down over Lockerbie in Scotland. Scottish police were "prohibited" by US agents from properly examining the crime scene for two whole days while those agents scoured the countryside for suitcases of heroin.)

History abounds with examples of governments peddling drugs. It should be no surprise therefore that the descendents of South American Indians decline to be lectured on the subject by brainless western politicians and policemen who appear to be shockingly unaware of their own governments misdeeds.

I turn now to the present matter. I have been offered immunity from prosecution on condition that I give evidence. My fiancé is Rudi who is an accused in this case. I should explain his nickname. He comes from Rudesheim in Germany and has non-activist socialist and perhaps Communist leanings. Jesus Maria Magdalene Peron gave him the nickname in a humorous reference to the German political activist "Red Rudi Dutske" in the

1960s. My Rudi has never taken part in any political activity whatsoever—far less killed anyone.
Before describing how I came to meet him perhaps I had better begin at the beginning as they say. Jesus Maria Magdalena Peron is my first cousin and is part of the extended family group who arrived in Berlin in 1990. I knew him from my earliest days. Let me paint a picture of him. To me as a small child he appeared flamboyantly brilliant, an outrageous creature. I suppose you would refer to him nowadays, in the modern overuse of every word and phrase so that it becomes debased, "as larger than life". He dominated everyone around him and not by means of physical strength (not that he lacked physical prowess) but by force of intellect. In my childish eyes he appeared to be omniscient. Jesus had the capacity to absorb new information on any subject like the proverbial sponge, analyse the same and then deploy seemingly irrefutable arguments in support of whatever position he had taken up on a subject. Even as a youth he appeared to me to be by turns urbane, sophisticated, civilised and witty and by turns brutally violent, insensitive to the needs and feelings of others and simplistic. He was something of a paradox.
Wearying of the ignorant jokes about his Christian names early in life, Jesus frequently alluded to aspects of his criminal career with New Testament analogies when in the company of intimate associates and friends.
Jesus absorbed much about his native Peru from his parents and appeared to have what psychologists call "cultural displacement".

Someone once said that an immigrant is a foreigner in two countries. Jesus was a perfect example of that. Perhaps that is why he never quite accepted his German nationality. None of our group did. Well, think about it. There we were-fluent German speaking Peruvians in the middle of Berlin! People sense rejection quickly even if this is never articulated.

Let me put thus. Dark skinned people of South American Indians are not fully paid up Germans. Yes I am aware that all European governments trumpet that their countries are "multi-racial" but that does not translate into reality on the ground. I do admit that many Europeans make valiant efforts to practise what their politicians preach.

Our sense of racial and cultural difference from native Germans soon found ways of expression. Thus it was that Jesus Maria Magdalena Peron was found by the Berlin police at the age of fourteen to be dispensing cocaine and other drugs to addicts outside The Kaiser Wilhelm church in the city centre. Jesus once released, humorously likened it to his New Testament's namesake conversing with the learned men in the Temple at the same age in that the episode displayed his precocious talents (for drug dealing that is rather than the exposition of Old Testament teaching!) It was not an altogether happy analogy.

Our group were agog and asked him where he had obtained such drugs. From my brothers in Peru was the answer.

There were no further incidents of drug dealing during his youth and Jesus settled into a German existence that even the most "hunde an der leine"

enthusiast among the worthy Burgers of Berlin would have found admirable. He qualified as a doctor in Berlin at the astonishingly young age of twenty-one and was marked out by the medical profession for a truly meteoric rise in their ranks. (Typically Jesus had much to say privately about the German medical profession and "the sons of Doctor Josef Mengele" as he referred to them as.) That said, he worked hard for nine years becoming a consultant at twenty-nine!
Then it happened. Jesus, ever the wit, announced that it was time to begin his "public ministry" and removed himself to Amsterdam.
The extended family found this decision strange, to say the least. By this time he was launched on a stellar career in medicine and being paid a substantial remuneration in comparison to most people if you discount the earnings by people in showbiz, pop stars and sportsmen and the like.
I did not hear from him for many months and the phone call I eventually received from him took me by surprise. After the customary pleasantries he invited me to Amsterdam there to enjoy a week entirely at his expense. I had by this time taken up gainful employment as a language teacher. Teaching world-wide is not renowned for its generous emoluments and I was only too delighted to accept his offer.
On arrival at Schipol airport and to my astonishment, I was met by rather swarthy gentleman. As I am Peruvian myself, I had little difficulty in concluding that my chauffeur rejoiced in the same ethnicity as myself. That said, I was

unable to feel any warmth for him: he was a thuggish, oafish looking specimen.

He conducted me to a somewhat opulent looking Mercedes, pale blue in colour and announced that he was under instructions from his master (Jesus) to give me a short guided tour of the city. As I had never set foot in Amsterdam before, I relaxed in one of the rear seats of the commodious limousine and allowed myself to be taken hither and thither. The old town of Amsterdam is not large when say compared with Berlin and thus acquiring a basic grasp of the layout is commensurately easy. If you realise that there are three principal canals, namely The Herren Gracht, The Prinzen Gracht and The Keyser Gracht all dating from "The Golden Age" in the 17th Century all you need to know in addition is that most of the main art galleries, concert hall (The Van Gogh, the Stedelijk, the Rijksmuseum and the Concertgebouw) are concentrated on the Museum Plein with The Hermitage being a short distance from these on the Waterlooplein.

What tourists refer to as the "city centre" need hardly detain any civilised being consisting as it does of Central Station, Damstraat, Dam Square and the Royal Palace (formerly The Town hall and not occupied by the Royal family who reside in The Hague.)

After this brief tour I was driven along the Museum Plein in competition with Tram Number Two to a solidly respectable district where my thuggish chauffeur intimated I would find Jesus ensconced in his house. By this time small alarm bells were beginning to sound in my head. From the outside the house occupied by Jesus was certainly not grand but it was solidly bourgeois (if not grand bourgeois.) Surely young doctors however brilliant had not made so much money by the age of 30? Have you won the lottery I enquired? Jesus laughed and replied that he had merely enjoyed success in business enterprises. What sort of businesses I could not help but murmur. He laughed once more and gestured across the road where there was a police station next to a Bistro called the Cafe des Amis. You see, he intoned; I live in a respectable neighbourhood.

He dismissed the chauffeur (presumably it was time for his next bunch of bananas) and led me into a commodious residence which as I have said, while not grand, was-how shall I describe it?-adequate.

I quickly took stock of my first cousin and his material possessions after he had settled me in a chair beneath two paintings which looked suspiciously Old Masters in provenance.

By this time in his life he was six feet two inches in height, slim, had a full head of jet black hair, a dark sallow complexion and large brown eyes mostly twinkling with amusement except when aroused by adversity. As Rudi has already said, in adversity the eyes of Jesus turned to the psychopathically emotionless eyes of a cobra snake.

Again as Rudi has said, his dress sense left much to be desired alternating as it did between what he considered to be "revolutionary chic"-army fatigues, boots and a green army or baseball hat-and a black suit for business matters with an incongruous red hat perched atop his unruly black locks. As regards the former mode of dress, he answered criticism by pointing out that wealthy

Chinese dressed in "revolutionary chic". They wore black jackets and Mao caps and as regards criticism of the second mode of dress by saying that he was, after all, a "businessman" and a black suit was entirely appropriate. Well out with it, I grumbled, what have you been up to the last few months? Concepcion, Concepcion, Jesus protested. You appear to be attempting to characterise me a criminal mastermind. It wouldn't surprise me, I retorted. I am nothing of the kind he replied with a breathtaking disregard for the truth as I was rapidly to discover. On he went. I had some savings as a doctor and in true entrepreneurial spirit invested them wisely. The risks I have taken have brought dividends. What did you invest in I demanded? A cafe just down from the Royal Palace and a shop on the Pieter Cornelius Hoofstraat. He paused. Listen, he suggested I play in a Peruvian street band and we have a gig tonight in Leidseplein. Why not freshen up and rest and then join us this evening? It's nothing grand. You'll enjoy it.

I can confirm that I first met Rudi in Leidseplein Square during one of Jesus's gigs. There is no paradox between the now fabulously wealthy Jesus the drug dealer and his continued participation as leader of a Peruvian pipe band. Peruvians love their indigenous music and entertaining those around them. If Jesus had a drug habit (and he was always clean during his life so far as I know), it was his music and the public performance of the same. Even during his occasional moments of depression

his music would lift his spirits immediately and transform him into an animated, exuberant soul.
I can still see Jesus in my mind's eye playing with his band in The Leidseplein in Amsterdam wearing his trademark red hat. (As a visible sign, he said, of "The Shining Path" of Peru. I do not think he was being serious). There he stood with a Havana cigar jammed between his teeth playing with his band. "Guantanamera" was always a popular ditty with the tourists of any nationality despite the chilling thought of the American Belsen there. (Yes he did know that Guantanamo is not in Peru but the tourists in Leidseplein didn't seem to know.)
The Square—the Leidseplein—lies on the intersection of several tram routes. I soon came to understand why the route of Tram Number Two was a vital artery in his "business activities".
It was on that very first night in Amsterdam that I sighted Rudi for the very first time and experienced an instant attraction. (I shall not stoop to cliché and describe it as "love at first sight"). Psychologists inform us that most human beings make up their minds about persons of the opposite gender within seconds. Upon mature reflection, I am of the opinion that that is so. If it is, then it is a somewhat melancholy thought that most young people are persuaded by their elders that examination of the other person's character is the paramount consideration together with such other extraneous matters such as "background", material prosperity and social standing. *A fortiori*, as the Latin has it (I am a teacher of languages as you will recollect), when one considers that those self same elder

persons have, in the days of their youth, surrendered to mere physical attraction themselves. Rudi appeared to be a man in his late twenties or even early thirties and, in a North European way, dark in colour without any hint of "mixed race" as today's police would call it.

I had already consumed two large glasses of wine and under the influence of those libations tilted my glass at Rudi who responded in like manner. By means of sign language he enquired whether it would be in order for him to join me at my table. Jesus did not miss this and called an immediate interval in his musical group's performance. A waiter, no doubt well used to the requirements of Jesus at interval time, appeared almost by magic at his side bearing a large Heineken beer. Thus armed Jesus returned to the table.

"Hola, Senor," he said good-naturedly to Rudi, conveying the beer to his lips with one hand and tipping his hat with the other. The fucking cheek of Jesus! I had scarcely had the opportunity to exchange a word with Rudi.

"*Te gusta la Mujer?*" he enquired in familiar South American Spanish. You like the woman?

The fucking cheek! He sounded like a clucking old hen.

"She is breathtaking," Rudi replied with commendable honesty.

I, *La Mujer* in question, began to feel as if I was some sort of slave girl being inspected prior to purchase.

The fucking cheek! He could not have failed to notice my anger at his intrusion and, Thank God, decided to withdraw.

"I have some more tunes to play for these good people," he said and gestured at the many souls populating the Leidseplein.

"I shall be through in some minutes and then you both must join me at The Uruguayan Steakhouse just off The Square."

However, at this point, the peace of The Kingdom of The Netherlands was disturbed by The British Army on "a night out". What pigs! They had had far too much to drink and wanted to sing "God Save The Queen" in competition, presumably to compete with the music on offer from Jesus and his band. The outcome of this clash was truly amusing. The soldiers were no match for Jesus and his band of wandering minstrels who were accomplished martial artists.

After a brief battle it was off to the restaurant.

The lawyers who are noting this statement of mine as part of the immunity deal are becoming agitated and would like me to describe the structure, organisation and resources of the organisation and its drug activities. You will recollect that I only arrived in Amsterdam after Jesus had set up his organisation. I cannot therefore describe what went on before I arrived.

Structurally Jesus ran a group called The Twelve Apostles. So far as I could see these men were key to the distribution of drug consignments in The Netherlands itself and beyond. It is entirely fair to describe all twelve men as the "muscle" of the organisation. To the last man they possessed oafish countenances with manners, or rather the lack of them, to boot.

To the extent that there was a headquarters for the organisation then I suppose that must be The Church of the Doubting Thomas on the Prinzen Gracht. The very name always makes me smile. No Spanish Church would be called after a doubting Thomas.
At this point let me point out and emphasise that there were no religious aspects to the organisation. Jesus and The Twelve Apostles were, of course, being Peru citizens from peasant stock, nominally Catholic but that is all they were. The Church had been deconsecrated. That is not uncommon in an age of falling congregations and declining financial resources. I gather that the more intellectually challenged persons in the prosecution team want to know what my role was in the organisation and if I held a "quasi-religious" role. This enquiry results from the prosecution team having discovered that Jesus referred to me as "The Sacred Feminine" and the rock upon which his church would be built. I, and others, have pointed out *ad nauseum* that Jesus was, by reason of the relentless harassment his name brought him at school in Berlin, given to the religious metaphor or analogy. I am his much loved first cousin but was never entrusted with any tasks beyond the mundane. It is true that he had designated me as his successor but as he had no plans to die immediately and was comparatively young and in rude good health I attached little importance to this pronouncement. Further, he took no steps to groom me for leadership.
That all said I cannot deny that I well knew that the consignments came in from the Middle East via Hungary, Romania, Austria, Switzerland and The

Czech Republic and then into Germany. I am happy to provide as much detail about these consignments as I can and have been told that I can do this once I have provided this overview of the organisation.

Suffice it to add at this stage that I was well aware of extensive consignments arriving from Spain originating there or in Morocco.

By far the most lucrative consignments were from Peru and elsewhere in South America and delivered by a Chinese network. Jesus told me very little about this part of his network.

I am asked at this juncture if I was ever aware of Jesus having a political "agenda". All I can say is that on one occasion he did tell me that one day he intended to return to his native land with sufficient funds to launch a political career. At no time did he outline a programme or agenda. I must say that I did not take him seriously and dismissed it as wishful thinking. He did however add that he expected his Chinese contacts to be useful. I do not wish to be unkind to my first cousin but the obvious lack of any concrete detail in his plan led me to the conclusion that he was a latter-day, day dreaming, would-be Che. Politically harmless I would say.

To return to the part I played in the organisation, my principal role was on the money laundering side of things. I ran the music shop known as "The Holy Sea" and occasionally helped out in the cafe and fast food restaurant downtown.

Those whom I knew well in the organisation were, of course, Rudi, Vanessa and her husband. I have met Maria de G... and Consuela M... and Agnes Le

B.... This may be difficult to believe but on those occasions when I met these persons we did not discuss "company business". In a high risk business it is downright dangerous to know more than you have to. Think about it. What I have said should have the ring of truth about it.

The only other person I met was that accursed mule whore Norma. I hate that girl and I will never be able to guarantee her safety. There are no words of condemnation strong enough to describe what she did. To save her own worthless skin she betrayed those whom I love. She was a poor little rich girl, a stinking spoiled brat, a worthless disease ridden whore who sold my people out. She sought to make money smuggling diamonds and when she got caught decided to betray us all.

In conclusion in this overview statement, I have only to add that I did know about the consignment coming in through Barcelona. Rudi told me. I played no part in the operation.

CHAPTER FIFTEEN
Extract of a statement made by Maria de G..., Spanish at Madrid Police Headquarters on May 5 2013

My full name is Maria de G... and I am forty three years of age. I provide this statement on the condition that has already been agreed upon between my lawyers and the prosecutors, namely that I shall be immune from prosecution in all time coming in the case against Jesus Maria Magdalena Peron in the Kingdom of The Netherlands and elsewhere.
I first met him on November 26 2012 in a former palacio in Madrid. This establishment is now a tango club much favoured by the aficionadas of the dance. It would be girlish and adolescent to deny being attracted to him. He appeared to be Hispanic and when I first saw him he was at one of the bars in the premises speaking to one of the girls employed there. I noted his confident ease of manner (always a characteristic which women find attractive in a man). He was dressed appropriately for a Tango club, that is to say he wore the ubiquitous double-breasted suit (de rigueur for Tango), a black shirt and white tie.
I took a table near to where he stood and I and my woman friend ordered drinks. In a short while I sensed his appraising eyes on me and I turned slightly and returned his gaze. He raised his glass and I reciprocated. Having no desire to be catalogued as a cheap slut by the policemen and lawyers who read this I should here point out that

social conventions are somewhat relaxed in a Tango Club. That is not to imply that sexual boundaries are crossed with greater ease than normally would be the case, merely that flirting is accepted as part of the dance culture.
He approached my table and asked if he might join us. I gave my consent. My woman friend sighed and made herself scarce with ill grace. He introduced himself as Jesus from The Kingdom of The Netherlands. Hispanic? I enquired. I'm tall, he replied and in the dark, handsome. It was difficult not to laugh at the old joke, such was the deadpan delivery. Yes, I'm Hispanic, he continued. I am originally from Peru. And you? De Madrid, I replied. And what do you do? I own a restaurant I answered (which was true even though I was very much a sleeping partner in the business.) At night though, I continued, I dress like a Tango tart and am something of a sexual predator when it comes to men. It was his turn to laugh.
We were getting on well together. (I believe the modern expression is "clicked".)
At the risk of appearing to give way to cliché and romantic sentiment, we, as they say, danced the night away. The vexed question arose as to whether to sleep together on the first date. At the risk of giving the impression of being a cheap Madrid slut, we did. I liked him. It was during the post-coital glow when, traditionally, a couple exchange information about each other that both of us enquired more deeply into each other's background.
As we all do on such occasions, he made much of his achievements in life, advising that he owned an

upmarket music shop on one of the most expensive streets in Amsterdam, on the P.C. Hoofstraat and further that he owned a cafe near the Royal Palace. He was pleased to advise that further, he owned a Maserati and a motor cruiser on the Rhine in Germany, this among other trinkets. Where is your main residence I enquired? I doss on Dam Square he joked before advising that his principal abode was a fine house in one of the more respectable areas of the city.
I am a woman of forty-three but I must confess that I became more excited by the moment about this man. He was clearly a man of substance as well as being very attractive. Next it would be my turn to disclose further details about myself. Realising that, I decided to make sure of him as best as any woman can.

After sex (for the second time)I began by sketching in details of my background, education and what my parents did except that my courage failed me at the last moment and I did not tell Jesus that my grandfather had served Franco well-rather too well as the readers of this statement will know all too well. I disclosed that I was not academically gifted and opted for business studies instead. Such was the financial position of my parents that they had put up the necessary collateral for my first and only business venture-a restaurant in one of the better districts of Madrid. Never marry? He asked. Never met anyone worthy of me, I replied. Many boyfriends? The usual loaded question! Statistically, I replied, a woman of my age has had six or seven partners. You make such assumptions as you wish

in that regard. So long as you have no communicable diseases, he murmured. I am not a whore, I retorted. Men!
Perhaps I should explain why I did not tell him what my grandfather did on that first occasion. It is obvious. I would have lost Jesus there and then. Why oh why do human beings hold others responsible for the sins of their fathers? War is a terrible thing but civil war plumbs such depths of cruelty that mere words are inadequate. Enough said about the business. After our first (rather steamy) date, we were almost inseparable. Inevitably, Jesus asked me to visit Amsterdam. It may sound strange for a woman of my background but I had never been there. But that was not the reason my pulses quickened as the plane began its descent into Schipol airport. As anyone who has ever lived should know, being "in love" can make you look a fool. I have no desire to reveal my innermost thoughts or feelings but I have to give some indication about what led me to become involved in serious international crimes.

I have been asked to narrate what I know of the operations of The Twelve Apostles in Amsterdam (whose "saviour" was Jesus Maria Magdalena Peron) Germany, France and The Netherlands and Spain. The answer is very little beyond what I knew of operations in Spain.
You must understand what a frightening creature Jesus could be. I can only describe him as being what I imagine a war-time agent to be. Ever alert, ever on guard, he missed nothing. To say he had in the words of the old cliché, "a sixth sense" would

be a travesty. Jesus had a seventh, an eighth and a ninth sense. I am unaware of him having been trained by the agencies of any State but he was, in my opinion, the equal of any such men or women. In consequence it will come as no surprise to the police and legal readers of my statement when I describe Jesus as a master of "compartmentalisation" that he is he had his "cells" in every country but none knew what the other was doing unless absolutely necessary. It was absolutely necessary that I knew about the consignment which the American and naval liaison officer was delivering in Barcelona by reason of its onward transhipment to Madrid and then Versailles. I therefore confirm that I knew that the consignment would be delivered to Consuela M... (the daughter of a United States Marine Officer) in Barcelona (what a rich irony!) and then handed to Vanessa S... at the Sagrada Familia and then brought here to Madrid and surrendered to Agnes and myself.
Agnes was a strange girl. She was fluent in Spanish, a student in Madrid and one of Rudi's conquests. He was the second most trusted lieutenant of Jesus (after me).
The parents of Agnes lived on a small estate in Versailles outside Paris. Once we had delivered the consignment to the family home (which Agnes always referred to as "the family seat"-a touch grandiose in my opinion!) the Amsterdam network would take over and convey the consignment to The Netherlands.
For the handover by Vanessa S... to myself and Agnes, Jesus had (true to character) selected a venue which I can only describe as outrageous—

The Ritz on the Paseo Prado. That said you can see his point. Anyone staying or visiting there is deemed to have certain respectability. I certainly did being the granddaughter of one of the Generalissimo's favourite generals.

So there you have my part in one of the principal criminal acts committed by Jesus and in which I was totally complicit.

Having taken delivery of drugs Agnes and I sped off to the Pyrenees and the French border in one of my cars, a Mercedes 600.

We travelled unchallenged by any officials of Customs or Police in either Spain or France. I am too well known to be challenged without there being a serious basis for the same.

I am asked why an apparently wealthy and well-connected woman would risk involvement in an international drug smuggling operation. I have already pointed out that love can make fools of us all. Perhaps it is true to say that prior to meeting Jesus I longed for some excitement in my life.

CHAPTER SIXTEEN
Extract of a statement given by Consuela M..., at police headquarters, Barcelona on 5 May 2013

My full name is Consuela M... and I am thirty years of age having been born in New York on 24 March 1983 only daughter of Major M... and Theresa Munoz. The parental address is West ...(number redacted) and Sixth Avenue.
I provide this statement to the authorities in Amsterdam on the basis that my lawyers have received a guarantee from them that I will receive a lighter sentence than my conduct would otherwise attract. This guarantee is part of a formal and written plea bargain.
I detested my father almost from the very first time I set eyes on him. He was a Major in the United States Marines, an occasional drunkard (the two appear to go together) and possessed a very small and totally closed mind. He was Hispanic-third generation.
I adored my mother Theresa who was Argentinean. She had had the misfortune to encounter my father while he was on a tour of duty at the embassy in Buenos Aires and married him.
There is nothing else of significance in my early life which is germane to the investigation in The Netherlands.
By 18 years of age I was fluent in Spanish, German and French, having inherited my mother's gift for

languages. On a summer's night during my eighteenth year and while my loathsome father was playing poker with some of his appalling military friends, I had a long discussion with my mother. I explained that I did not want to take up my place at one of the Ivy League universities immediately. My opinion was that I would benefit from a gap year and put some distance between myself (literally) and my loathsome progenitor. Your father will be displeased, she observed unnecessarily, but I agree with you. If you are certain that that is what you want to do it she said, do it now and with not a word to him. Will you be OK? Yes, was my reply. I shall tell him that I had no idea what you were planning, my mother said. He will rage for several days and that will be in the end of it.

Three days later and with a gift of $6000 from my mother I was on my way to Peru, there to begin what turned into an odyssey lasting several years. I travelled widely in South America, securing employment where I could. My mother and I met from time to time in Cuba where my father would not dare to venture.

Eventually I met and married an English artist then on a working holiday in Ecuador. It was a mistake. I had sacrificed my independence for a man I did not love. We settled in Barcelona.

Ah Barcelona! To a small extent it provided compensation for a loveless marriage. The City of Gaudi, The Sagrada Familia, the Placa Catalunya, Ramblas, the Gothic Quarter and the seafront!

It was on a return flight from London to meet my mother (she was there on a cheap holiday trip) that I met the man who was a close associate of Jesus

Maria Magdalena Peron. I had noticed him in the departure lounge and when it transpired that it was a quiet flight I found myself almost unconsciously taking a seat in the same row as him.
Preliminary information about each other was rapidly exchanged. He was German. (To my surprise, I must say. I thought he was either Spanish or of Spanish extraction.) To my credit I suppose, I did tell him that I was married. (I could hardly deny it given the ring on my finger.) That said, I was well aware of the feeling that it would take very little to make myself available to him.
I asked him what he did for a living. He replied that he was a musician by training and worked as when he could find musical engagements. Otherwise he worked as a general *factotum* to the head of a company in Amsterdam. This company he said had an eclectic prospectus dealing in medicinal products, a cafe in downtown Amsterdam and a musical shop on of the city's more expensive streets. At no time did he as much as hint at the company being a front for the international peddling of drugs.
And so the flight to Barcelona passed pleasantly in small talk and idle conversation about such diverse matters as the prevailing weather in London and Barcelona and the vicissitudes in the fortunes of the city's most famous football club.
As the plane came into land I formed the impression that he was reluctant to part company with me (an emotion I shared for him.) The solution lay in our sharing a taxi into town. We then had to come up with a solution to the problem as to how we could meet again. (This was

all caused by my having pointed out that I was married.) Rudi solved this problem. He advised that while it was not his first visit to the city he would welcome the tutored eye of a resident and thus adjudge it an honour and a privilege if I would lunch with him tomorrow. But of course I said demurely as a woman of unimpeachable moral rectitude would.

We met the following day just before 1 pm at a restaurant in the old Gothic Quarter which enjoyed my culinary approval.
I do not recollect how or when the subject of drugs first cropped up in conversation. Perhaps it was the wine consumed that day combined with being on a date with someone to whom I was attracted which renders my recollection rather imprecise. My best recollection is that it was on that first date that he mentioned at some point that he used soft drugs recreationally. This is not a criminal offence in Spain provided that the drugs used are for personal use only. Making mention in conversation in Spain that you use soft drugs recreationally is not what anyone under the age of forty would regard as a "conversation stopper". It would cause no more furore than saying you like having a few drinks.
The next few days in Barcelona are best described as halcyon. I struggled to dismiss notions of embarking on the cliché "whirlwind romance" but he was fun to be with and the excitement was all the more intense because I was still married then. What did we do in those first few days? Well, apart from the obvious we tended to stick to the better restaurants (and only those restaurants within

walking distance of a hotel bedroom.) Rudi had money to spend. As I have said, he told me that he was a classically trained musician but had not been good enough as a soloist to make it on the concert hall circuit. He had to settle for gigs among the musical ensembles of Amsterdam, jazz gigs and session music work for the morons in the pop world who can't play an instrument for toffee. Apart from his musical activities, Rudi said he made good money for a business man whom he worked for in Amsterdam. I don't think Rudi ever named this man and nor did I ask. If I remember correctly all Rudi said about the business this man ran was that it was something to do with medicinal products.

Even in those early days Rudi would ask me to deliver packages to his friends when he was busy with work commitments (or so he said). When I asked what was in the packages, he would jokingly say it was just some "Charley". With the value of hindsight I doubt if he was joking.

I may appear stupid and naive or, alternatively, I may simply not be believed but it was in that casual manner that I became a drug courier or mule. In my view investigators of drug crimes are all too disposed to seeing couriers or mules as hardened criminals when, in my experience, they are poor, stupid, deluded fools like myself. I suppose you could say that I became Rudi's main agent in Barcelona but it certainly did not feel like that at the time.

I have been asked to further describe my activities on Rudi's behalf later as, I am told, there is a degree of urgency in procuring as much evidence as possible about the twenty-five kilograms of cocaine brought in by an American naval and liaison officer a few days ago. I am asked to describe my part in this operation.

Here is my account. Rudi phoned me at home the day before. (I was still living with my husband.) Rudi sounded tense and asked me to meet him for a glass of wine and coffee in the Placa Catalunya in the centre of town. I made some excuse to my husband about having to console a broken hearted girlfriend after a failed romance and shot out the door.

If Rudi had sounded tense on the phone, his appearance at the cafe in which we had arranged to meet only provided confirmation of my suspicion. He spoke softly-so much so that I had difficulty hearing what he had to say at times. He was also quite theatrical in his conduct and glanced around him frequently. He told me that an American naval officer would bring a consignment of drugs into Barcelona the following evening. Rudi explained that he wanted me to play only a small part in the delivery. I had heard enough and also had been alarmed by Rudi's demeanour that at first I refused. Stupid as it sounds Rudi could be persuasive. He explained that the arrangements for the delivery of the consignment had already been made and that the naval officer expected to be met by a girl. I would only be in his company for a short while until the consignment was handed over. If anything went wrong Rudi said and we were apprehended, he would immediately surrender himself to the authorities. Please don't laugh but I believed him!

The following day in the Plaza Mayor I watched with a disgust I could not conceal as the American in navy uniform appeared and made towards me. (It will be recalled that I hated my marine officer father.) To any disinterested observer, I suppose the little scene we created appeared just as intended, another man in uniform making a play for a girl. Conversation between us was minimal. Exchange of pre-arranged ID over, the officer intimated that he had parked his van down at the Customs headquarters near the Barcelona shoreline. Breathtaking insolence! A van parked with twenty-five kilograms of Charley in the boot at Customs headquarters!

Conform to the instructions Rudi had given me I kept the pre-arranged rendezvous with Vanessa S... that night at 11pm and but a stone' throw from the Sagrada Familia. Vanessa is the only other person in the organisation I have ever met apart from Rudi and the lower mules. I did not care much for this girl. She was in temperament "vivacious" or "bubbly" as today's frivolous women are wont to describe such a personality. That was the difficulty I had with her. International drug smuggling is, at the risk of providing a glimpse of the blindingly obvious, a dangerous business. I did not approve of a girl with such a spontaneous character being put in harm's way. In my opinion a more calculating disposition is what is required. She was given to ill-considered judgements which could imperil those around her. That said Rudi thought the world of her and frequently deployed her to Barcelona. Vanessa was from Madrid of course but had an ageing aunt in Barcelona. This provided the excuse to run between the two cities and Amsterdam. The system in Spain up until this point had been that I was the central collecting point for all incoming consignments from Morocco and the Costas. From Barcelona couriers or mules travelled by various means to Amsterdam. However when an unusually large consignment was due in Barcelona, usually Vanessa was despatched and such a consignment was then conveyed personally by her to Madrid. (I did not know this at the time but I have been given to understand that Jesus Peron, whom I had never heard of but, I am informed, was the boss of the whole organisation, had a woman associate there of some influence.) You always knew that the consignment was large because not only did Vanessa arrive in Barcelona but she was accompanied by the doormat she had for a husband. He was a serving police officer in the police of Amsterdam. My impression of him was that he never enquired too deeply into his wife's activities presumably on the basis that he benefited financially or was otherwise remunerated. I personally always heaved a sigh of relief when, having flown into Barcelona, they departed for Madrid in a hired campervan. I understand that her husband would make much of his Amsterdam police badge if they were stopped for some minor road traffic demeanour (and she would make much of the fact that she had graduated from the University of Madrid with a degree in law.) By those means they were never required to submit the vehicle to a thorough search. I vastly preferred

dealing with the smaller consignments sent by the couriers from Amsterdam.
Conversation with Vanessa that night at the Sagrada Familia was, as usual, kept to a minimum. Being a girl from Madrid Vanessa, of course, found time to make some caustic comments about the Catalans. She really was insufferable at times-well, all the time. I, for my part, could not resist reminding her that the citizens of Barcelona had run out of Champagne on the night of the Generalissimo's death; such was the mood of celebration. With one or two other exchanges of traditional, vituperative comments indicating that the distrust and hatred between Castille and Catalan was alive and well, I watched them depart into the night in a campervan and on returning to my apartment poured and gratefully sipped a large glass of wine.
As I have said, the only two people in the "senior echelons" of the organisation whom I met were Rudi and Vanessa. I will furnish names and addresses of the lesser fry who acted as couriers or mules between Barcelona and Amsterdam.

CHAPTER SEVENTEEN
On 6 May 2013 at the 13 court of Untersuhungsrichter, Aachen, Germany.
Evidence of Vanessa S....

Untersuhungsrichter, Aachen (hereinafter "U"): Well, Good Morning everyone and especially to Senora –or is it Senorita?—Vanessa S.... I'm never very sure when to address a Spanish woman as Senora or senorita.
Vanessa S... (Hereinafter VS): I am a married woman, Sir, so "Senora" is the correct mode of address.
U: Thanks for that. Well, welcome to Aachen, Senora. Now may I say word about procedure, Senora. Legal procedure here is a different from what you see on television and the movies. We are quite relaxed here and don't have all the pomp and circumstance of British courts—wigs and gowns and all that crap. I think it is because the British have a Queen and aristocracy. They all like dressing up and parading up and down. Nor do we have all the drama of American courts if there be a smidgeon of truth in the TV dramas I watch. Is that clear?
VS: Yes Sir.
U: Our procedure is inquisitorial and not adversarial. We don't need dramas Now then, as I understand matters, and nobody tells me very much. I'm just a judge and often feel like a mushroom-kept in the dark and fed on...

(Note: laughter in court.)
Now, where was I? Ah yes. As I understand matters you and your husband who is an Amsterdam policeman fled last night across what we used to call a border before the Schengen Treaty. Ever heard of that? No? Well let me recommend it to you Senora if ever you can't get to sleep at night. It's a cure for insomnia as all European law is. I'm not supposed to say that.
(Note: laughter in court)
Now then where was I? Ah yes, you and your policeman husband fled across what we used to call a border and then the Dutch authorities-I don't like the Dutch very much, do you?-asked that you be arrested. On what grounds I'm not very sure...
(Note: laughter in court)
...but there we are and the Staatsanwalt here tells me you have committed a crime here. So that's why you and I have the pleasure of each other's company this morning. Perhaps you might care to start at the beginning and tell me how you came to be in The Netherlands and then fled to Germany. Let me give you a word of warning. It is now 11.15 and I always adjourn my court at 12.45 punctually so that I can partake of luncheon. There is usually only some ghastly North German dish on the menu. We are not renowned for our cuisine in Germany...
(Note: laughter in court.)
VS: I was born and brought up in one of the Barrios in Madrid
U: A Barrio you say...what is that?
VS: It means a district, Sir. It is generally taken to refer to a working class district. May I continue?

U: Of course, of course.
VS: I worked hard at school and somehow managed to gain entry to the law school in the University of Madrid passing all exams with distinction.
U: Goodness! I hope our Staatsanwalt heard that. Frau Lemper?
Frau Ute Lemper: I heard what the Senora said.
U: There will be no need to detain the young lady until the determination of proceedings?
Frau Ute Lemper: In the circumstances, no.
U: I am pleased to hear it. Our German prisons are filled with such riff-raff. Please continue, Senora.
VS: You must understand, Sir that life in Spain in the last 5-6 years has been difficult.
U: It's not been a great deal of fun in Germany either, what with having to pay for bail-outs for the Greeks, Portuguese, Italians, the Irish and indeed, it pains me to say so, Senora, your own dear country. I really do wish all these people would stop eating olives, drinking wine and doing "Zorba the Greek" dances. Why can't they all do a decent days work as we do in Germany?
VS: The Barrios, Sir, have become quiet. They used to hum with life but so many have no money and no jobs. In Spain, you only get unemployment for two years and then you are on your own. As a group, people in the position I have described are known as "**Los Indignados**".
U: Yes I have heard that expression in news reports.
VS: Politicians in our country and yours suggest that we should leave the country of our birth and

find work elsewhere in Europe. Many of us find that hard to do when it is not our fault.
U: I have sympathy with your plight.
VS: Despite an excellent academic record, I could not find work. I and my family have humble origins. We know no-one in a position of influence who could open doors for me.
U: So you decided to come to the Netherlands?
VS: Yes. I had a girl friend there who was beginning to make a comfortable living for herself. I hesitate to tell you what she did for a living.
U: I can guess. Let me assure you that I will not be judgemental.
VS: (Note: crying.) She worked as an upmarket call girl.
U: Please don't distress yourself, Senora S....
VS: The important thing was that she had an apartment of her own and was willing to put me up and feed me until I could find work.
(Note: Hiatus of several moments while Senora S... composed herself.)
VS: You see how far we Spanish have fallen.
U: Would you like an adjournment of the proceedings so that you can compose yourself?
VS: That will not be necessary. Finding work in The Netherlands was not easy either. They have their problems there to. I ended up touring cafes and Bistros asking-perhaps begging would be a better word-if there were any vacancies for waitresses. It was so disheartening. One day and I walked into a cafe cum bistro called the Cafe des Amis on Marystraat which is on the fringes of a park in the city called the Vondel Park.

U: Mmmn. Know it well. Slept the night there when I was a student and very drunk.
(Note: laughter in court.)
VS: Having found employment-and you do not know how terrifying it is to be without a job and money...
U: Actually, I do. I was sacked from my first job as a lawyer for taking too great an interest in one of the secretaries...
(Note: laughter in court.)
VS: ...I began to relax a little and sleep well for the first time in months. I liked Amsterdam and there is, after all, a long history shared by the Spanish and The Netherlands with a large Spanish presence there today...
U: Really? I didn't know that. Can you elaborate?
VS: ...Yes Sir. In the 16th century, The Duke of Burgundy who had acquired The Low Countries through a mixture of astute inter-marriage and expedient alliances bequeathed The Low Countries including The Netherlands to the King of Spain...
U: Just like that, eh? I do so wish that on my own death I could bequeath to my children say... Nord Rhein Westphalia...
(Note: laughter in court.)
 U...Come to think of it, who would want to inherit Nord Rhein Westphalia? ...
(Note: more laughter in court.)
VS: It was through work that I met my husband. There is a police station almost next to the Cafe des Amis and some of the policemen, depending on their work commitments, would drop in from time to time during their break for a coffee. He was a solid, dependable man...

U: ...but you didn't love him?

VS: No, I didn't love him. Then Rudi started to visit the Cafe des Amis.

U: This is the Rudi the Dutch authorities have been going on about?

VS: I would imagine so. He was very funny as well as being physically attractive...

U: And you did love him?

VS: Yes. I remember the first time we met. While serving him a coffee and a sandwich I remarked that he must be lucky in the job he had...out and about on a sunny day rather than being cooped up in an office. He said he was the driver of the Number two tram which runs outside the Cafe des Amis. It was the way he said it. It seemed funny at the time. He told me he was a musician and when not playing gigs worked as a factotum for a businessman in Amsterdam.

U: Any mention of drugs?

VS: No, that came later. He turned up perhaps three times a week after that and we became accustomed to kissing each other three times on the cheek when we met (following the Dutch custom.) The next bit in the story makes me look cheap...

U: No-one will laugh or snigger, Senora.

VS: One morning, when the Cafe des Amis had little custom and we had exchanged greetings in the customary manner and...I don't know what came over me...but I told him that the zip of my skirt was giving me trouble and could he possibly try to rectify the matter? Of course, he replied. I am a Gentleman. Best that we try to sort it in the staff loo otherwise the solitary customer of The Cafe des

Amis might think that we are on terms of intimacy, he advised. You can guess what happened...
U: We can.
VS: In the weeks that followed, intimacy occurred in cars, hotel beds and occasionally in the staff loo of the Cafe des Amis. He decided to recruit me. Rudi knew that we-my husband and I-were hard up what with the shocking cost of housing in Amsterdam and day-to-day living expenses. I can't remember exactly what was said but he offered me 2000 Euros to deliver a parcel to Rotterdam.
U: Did he say what was in the parcel?
VS: No Sir. You may find it hard to believe but he never told me what was in it just that the contents were very valuable.
U: But you had a good idea that the contents of the parcel were drugs?
VS: Yes. Over the next few weeks he gave me many other packages to deliver...
U: Where were these packages delivered to?
VS: Different places. I delivered packages sometimes to Rotterdam, sometimes here in Amsterdam itself and now again to here in Aachen.
U: How much did your husband know about these matters?
VS: He knew everything.
U: Including the affair you were having with Rudi?
VS: Yes. Life can be complicated. At the risk of sounding cheap, the money was good. Sometimes, as I said, it was as much as 2000 Euros...
U: A proportion of which was for...how shall I put it..."services" rendered...by you personally to Rudi?
VS: Yes.

U: And this was all happening under the very noses of the police?
VS: Yes.
U: And indeed with the connivance of the police in the personage of your husband?
VS: Yes.
U: You realise that your position is very serious?
VS: Yes.
U: What else can you tell us about this matter?
VS: Across the street from the police station, Rudi's boss had his house.
U: Is that the man referred to in the Dutch documents as Jesus Maria Magdalena Peron?
VS: Yes.
U: Describe this man to me.
VS: A man in his thirties, Hispanic looking...
U: He came from Peru I believe?
VS: Yes. He is very good-looking, flamboyant, larger than life, by turns morose and withdrawn and by turns extrovert, witty...
U: I think I have the picture.
VS: His dress sense could be spectacularly awful. It was either a black suit for serious business meetings or military fatigues with a baseball hat, beret or a red hat...
U: A red hat?
VS: ...sometimes. Usually a cigar stuck in his mouth.
U: Sounds like a Che Guevara look alike.
VS: Exactly. He was a doctor too. Over a period of a few months I was slowly allowed into the centre of operations namely his house...
U: Overlooking the police station?
VS: Yes.

U: Did your husband know about all of this?
VS: He knew about the house and Jesus but he had no idea of the extent of operations.
U: That's at least something. Well, it's 1245 everyone and time for me to be fed. Are you joining me for lunch Frau Lemper? Don't look so surprised, Senora S.... Judges and lawyers often eat together at German courts. We promise not to discuss your case. There will be no need for you to feel envious of us either. I can assure you that the canteen food here is appalling. It's worse than prison food. Do you know what's on the menu today? You don't? Let me tell you. The soup is Eintopf. Do you know what kind of soup that is? You don't? Let me tell you it is the most disgusting pigswill you could encounter...
(Note: laughter in court.)
...and then the main course is bratwurst and potato...you would think that we were pigs...Honest I wouldn't be a judge except that I need the money...
(Note: laughter in court.)

S: Good afternoon, everyone. Well, Frau Lemper and I had the most appalling lunch and the only good thing about it being afternoon is that in three hours time I will be at home with my beloved and being properly fed. Now Senora Vanessa S..., I think you were about to tell us what you knew about this drug smuggling business?
VS: Yes, Sir. I didn't know everything.
U: Just tell us what you did know.
VS: Well, Sir, while much of the planning and some of the dealing took place at the house Jesus had at

the Vondel Park, he owned other properties and businesses in the city which were no more than fronts for drug dealing. The office headquarters of his business empire was The Church of the Doubting Thomas in the Prinzen Gracht...
U: Gracious! Was Jesus dishing out drugs during church services?
VS: Let me explain Sir. The premises had been a church...
U: Thank Goodness!
VS: ... and converted to office space...
U: Thank Goodness! So only the edifice looked like a church?
VS: Not quite, Sir. Jesus left the interior of the church as it was...
U: You mean there were still an altar and a pulpit?
VS: Yes, Sir but the altar now had a number of flat screen computers on it and the pulpit had a springboard diving board attached...
U: Whatever for?
VS: Men who double-crossed Jesus were forced to "walk the plank" as it were...
U: I'm beginning to think that I'm losing my mind...
Note: (laughter in court)
...Senora S..., are you certain this was a drug smuggling organisation and not some Satan worshippers' outfit?
VS: It gets worse, Sir. The most trusted hoodlums Jesus had—usually South American—were called the twelve Apostles and meetings were held at the high altar. Jesus would insist that they place their Glock pistols on the High Altar so that he could see them...

U: I am losing my mind. Did you attend these meetings?
VS: No Sir but I was present at the start of one meeting.
U: Tell us what you remember.
VS: The twelve apostles were at the high altar with their Glock pistols in plain view. There was a knock at the front door of the Church and Jesus himself went to see who it was...
U: ...And who was it?
VS: An elderly Dutch couple, Sir.
U: And what did they want? Drugs?
VS: No Sir. They said they had been abused in the Church 50 years ago by the clergy and wanted to visit in order to try and find closure...
U: So what happened?
VS: Jesus told them to fuck off.
U: Almighty God!
VS: Jesus then came back to the altar and called Roberto a cunt...
U: One moment Senora. I am not yet familiar with the dramatis personae in this case.
VS: Roberto was a Columbian...
U: Was?
VS: I think Jesus killed him Sir.
U: What for?
VS: He lost ten kilograms of cocaine at Schipol airport, Sir.
U: Senora S.... I would have thought that as your boss's name was Jesus and you were all in a church, he might at least have offered Roberto confession before proceeding to execution...
(Note: laughter in court.)
...what happened next?

VS: I was told to fuck off by Jesus.
U: And you did?
VS: Yes Sir, I did. May I continue Sir?
U: Yes.
VS: The only other businesses I knew about in Amsterdam were his cafe near the Royal Palace and his music shop on the Cornelius Straat.
U: OK, describe what went on in these businesses.
VS: I was only in the cafe a few times Sir and didn't have anything to do with the running of it.
U: I take it when you say it was a cafe you mean a cafe in the Amsterdam sense of the word?
VS: Yes Sir. It sold cannabis products. I'm only guessing but I don't think it made a lot of money-at least not in comparison Jesus's other sources of income. I think that it was one of the many means by which he laundered the profits from his drug dealing. You must understand Sir that you can run out of ways in which to launder money.
U: I have never made enough money to have that kind of problem.
VS: Once you have exhausted the numbered Swiss accounts, the accounts in Luxemburg, Lichtenstein...
U: Alright, alright, don't remind me how poor I am...
VS: ...you need some legitimate businesses in order to...
U: I've got the picture, Senora.
VS: Jesus owned an up market music shop in the P.C. Hoofstraat, Amsterdam. It's an expensive street.
U: What did he sell there?

VS: Expensive musical instruments, Bosendorfer pianos...
U: I'm in the wrong line of work. I've only got an upright piano...
(Note: laughter in court.)
VS: ...and some Strads...
U: Good God!
VS: Again the shop was just a front for money laundering.
U: Can you describe the money laundering aspects of this organisation in any detail?
VS: I'm sorry Sir but I wasn't allowed near that side of the business but I can describe some of the organisation's activities in Germany and Spain.
U: A real multinational company you worked for...
(Note: laughter in court)
...OK, begin with Germany.
VS: Jesus kept a powerful motor cruiser berthed near Cologne to be used when he found stress too much for him...
U: ...as you do...
VS: It was called "The Shining Path"...
U: Isn't that the name for some sort of terrorist outfit in South America?
VS: I think they see things differently, Sir.
U: I'm sure they do. In the days of my youth, I used to be something of a terrorist. I was a member of the Green Party...
(Note: laughter in court.)
...carry on Senora.
VS: Well, Sir, he was very fond of cruising down the Rhine to Koblenz, to "The German Corner".
U: Whatever for?
VS: Well, Sir. Jesus was given to machismo...

U: He would, being a Peruvian person...
VS: ...and he saw Kaiser Wilhelm the First's statue there as a statement of a macho man...
U: ...I'm sure Kaiser Bill did too...I can't stand the Prussians myself...
(Note: laughter in court.)
VS: But there was another reason for his cruises south to Koblenz...
U: Do tell.
VS: ...one of the principal drug smuggling routes from the Middle East, Hungary, the Czech republic and the like is through the south of Germany, the Bodensee and the like...
U: Oh no. I have a weekend house there...
VS: And Jesus liked to keep an eye on his mules from a distance. Koblenz is a railway hub and most of the mules made for there. Jesus felt that once the mules were on the train at Koblenz, he could relax. And, if anything went wrong he could pick them up and take them back on his cruiser...
U: Nice of him.
VS: Jesus loved German railways...
U: Why was that?
VS: He once told me that he greatly admired how the Germans moved several million men by railway as the First World War broke out...
U: Why did he admire that?
VS: Machismo Sir.
U: Next you'll being telling me that Jesus liked Wagner...
VS: He did, Sir.
(Note: laughter in court.)
I don't know anything more about the German end of the business.

U: OK, before we get on to the Spanish end of the business, let's adjourn until tomorrow morning. 930 sharp everyone.

U: Good Morning everyone. Please sit down. Now Senora S..., I hope you slept well or as well as you could in the circumstances.
VS: Thank you Sir.
U: Now Senora, the Spanish end of the business. What can you tell us about that?
VS: The main collecting point Sir, for drug consignments originating from Morocco and the Costas was Barcelona. Rudi's main agent there, Sir, was a girl called Consuela M.... She is an American citizen but obviously of Spanish descent...
U: ...obviously...
VS: Most of the consignments were not large and usually couriers or mules from Amsterdam were despatched to Barcelona to uplift them and convey them back to Amsterdam. That said, whenever a large consignment arrived in Barcelona from wherever, I was sent to bring it back...
U: ...Why was that?
VS: I think it was a question of trust, Sir.
U: You were highly regarded by Jesus Peron and Rudi?
VS: Yes Sir. And I had a perfectly good reason for being in Barcelona and Madrid...
U: I know that your parents reside in Madrid but what perfectly good reason had you for visiting Barcelona on a frequent basis?
VS: I have an ageing aunt there, Sir.
U: I see. So how did you travel to Barcelona?
VS: By plane, Sir.

U: But surely you did not fly back with a drug consignment?
VS: No, Sir. My husband and I...
U: Your husband travelled with you to Barcelona to uplift drug consignments?
VS: Yes Sir but I never told him what the real purpose of the trips to Barcelona was...
U: But surely he must have entertained suspicions at the very least?
VS: Yes, Sir but he never asked any questions.
U: Does wilful blindness appear to be an adequate description of your husband's conduct?
VS: I suppose so Sir...
U: There is no supposing about it, Senora, surely?
(Note: Vanessa S... did not answer this question.)
VS: Our practice, Sir was to rendezvous with Consuela M......
U: Where?
VS: It varied, Sir but the Sagrada Familia was a popular place for rendezvous...
U: Religion and places of Christian worship appear to have been important to you people.
VS: We would take custody of the consignment and travel by hired car to Madrid...
U: Did you never worry about being stopped and searched by the Spanish police even say on suspicion of having committed a minor road traffic demeanour?
VS: We calculated that our car would not be searched.
U: How so?
VS: My husband always carried his police badge with him...

U: Ah.
VS: And, Sir, I like to think that I have a pleasing Madrid manner about me. On the few occasions we, were, as they say, pulled over, I would always find a way to tell the police that I had graduated with distinction in my law studies at the University of Madrid..
U: Senora, I have to say that your position in this matter is becoming ever more serious. Do you wish to continue?
VS: Yes, Sir.
U: Very well. Now the Dutch authorities appear to be much exercised by events in Barcelona a few days ago. Do you want to tell me about that occasion?
VS: Yes, Sir. Jesus had managed in recent weeks to recruit an American naval and liaison officer. He liaised with the American drug agencies and was a frequent visitor to South American countries and Europe. Naturally, with his high level security clearance it was comparatively easy for him to smuggle drugs out of any country and into another.
U: Having regard to the papers presented by the Dutch authorities to this court, can you confirm that this man was Lieutenant Commander Alaska of the United States Navy?
VS: Yes, Sir. He arrived in Barcelona a few days ago carrying a consignment of twenty-five kilograms of pure cocaine. It had a street value in Europe of many millions of Euros. Jesus himself flew down to Barcelona with Rudi to oversee matters. Consuela M... was instructed to meet him in the Plaza Major and then go with him to where the consignment was...

U: Why was that? Why did you not have the officer hand over the consignment directly to you?

VS: Jesus wanted to make sure that the officer was not the subject of surveillance. The calculation of Jesus was that if the consignment of the drug was handed to an intermediary before being surrendered to me then any surveillance would be manifest.

U: I see. Please continue.

VS: The consignment was transferred to the campervan which my husband and I had hired and we left for Madrid.

U: Where in Madrid did you take the consignment to?

VS: The Ritz where we met a well-to-do woman associate of Jesus Peron. Her name is Maria de G....

U: What can you tell me about this woman?

VS: Her grandfather was one of Franco's favourite generals. Her mother is something of a grandee and owns one of the larger estates near Toledo.

U: How did Jesus Peron come to know her?

VS: They met, Sir, at a former palacio in Madrid which now caters for Tango aficionados. The lady is well known in Madrid and Spanish society.

U: Not the sort of lady one would expect to smuggle drugs, I imagine.

VS: Precisely, Sir. Waiting for us there was a young lady who was a courier or mule recruited by Rudi.

U: And what is her name?

VS: Agnes Le B..., Sir.

U: French?

VS: Yes, Sir. She is from Versailles. Her parents own a small estate there. They are well known vets and Agnes studied that science in Madrid which, as

you may know Sir, is a world-renowned institute for the study of that subject. Agnes got to know the family through field work on the estate outside Toledo.
U: So what happened to the consignment?
VS: It was handed over Sir and then both women left in a large Mercedes.
U: Belonging to the lady I assume?
VS: I think so Sir.
U: And what did you and your husband do?
VS: We dropped our hired car in Madrid Sir and then flew back to Amsterdam.
U: Anything else you'd like to tell us?
VS: No, Sir. That's about it. I can name many of the small-time couriers and mules but I can add nothing else about the organisation's structure and personnel.
U: Well, Senora, you will know yourself that what you have told me discloses participation in such serious crimes that I am unable to assist you regain your liberty...
VS: I understand Sir.
U: You will have to go to a higher court to appeal for your liberty. Well, that's about it Senora. Thank you for your honesty.

CHAPTER EIGHTEEN
Statement given by Agnes to her lawyer in Versailles on May 7, 2013

"Thank you for seeing me at such short notice."
"Think nothing of it. We have acted as lawyers for your family for as long as I can remember."
"I am in very serious trouble..."
"I am certain it cannot be as bad as that..."
"It is. I am, as they say, "on the run". I want to make a sworn statement."
"What about?"
"It will rapidly become apparent what the matter is about."
"Normally I would not consider taking a sworn statement from a client when I do not know what the subject of..."
"Please. We must not waste time. The police may track me down at any time."
"Very well. Let's keep things simple. I will administer the oath of verity. You should then state your full name, date of birth and place of residence. Next you should say what you want to say. Be precise, succinct and do not stray from the points you want to make. Avoid circumlocution and euphemism and above all else have in the forefront of your mind that making a sworn statement can have serious legal consequences-usually prison-if anything in your statement is found to be false and to a material degree. Do you fully understand what I have said?"
"Yes."

"As far as you are aware-and I have to ask this-are you of sane and sober senses and do you make this statement of your own free will?"
"Yes."
"Lastly I shall interrupt you only when a point requires elucidation or clarity. Do you understand?"
"Yes."
"Very well. Let us begin. State your full name, date of birth, place of residence and occupation."
"My full name is Agnes Le B.... I am 23 years of age having been born at Versailles on 19 February 1990 and reside at Le B... estate, Versailles. I have just completed my studies at the School of vetinery sciences. Last year in Madrid at the Queen Sofia art gallery I met a young German called Rudi..."
"Surname please?"
"I shall provide his full name and address later. Please let me speak."
"He gave me to understand that he was in Madrid on a business trip. He did not specify precisely what sort of business he was in. He was amusing and not unattractive. When he suggested that the weekend would be more fun if he had a local guide, namely me, to accompany him, I could see no reason to reject the offer. We went to the usual tourist attractions in Madrid where, predictably, he enquired what a girl from Versailles thought about Royalty. In my experience, almost everyone asks this question of me when I tell them where I come from. I gave my usual, much practised reply that Madame Guillotine had been retired much too early. He was amused as everyone is when I give this reply.

Over lunch at one of Madrid's over-priced restaurants, he told me more about himself. Rudi was born and brought up in Rudesheim in Germany. When he was 18 he embarked on classical musical training in Cologne. Not good enough for a career as a soloist, he did not want to become orchestra fodder and now played wherever he could in classical ensembles or jazz gigs, sometimes even as a session musician for pop artists. He supplemented his income by acting as a factotum for a businessman in Amsterdam.
"Did he make mention of drugs?"
"Hardly, we had only just met."
"Forgive the interruption."
"The businessman's portfolio of interests was eclectic ranging from the ownership of a high-end shop selling musical instruments, a cafe and a company dealing in medicinal products. Next it was my turn to give him some information about myself. I kept it to a minimum telling him that my parents were well off vets who had accumulated enough money to buy a small estate outside Versailles and that I was in the process of completing my studies in Madrid. To cut a long story short, I slept with him that night. He was very honest about his private life and told me that he had two other girl friends whom he slept with from time to time. It was only to be expected and I did not pursue the matter beyond registering the fact that one girl was Spanish (but not living in Madrid) and the other American. He invited me to visit Amsterdam (I surmised that both the other girls had been through this process and asked if my

proposed visit to the city would cause him any difficulties in his private life. He foresaw none.) I had been in Amsterdam several times in the past and in consequence would not describe myself as a tourist when I went to spend a weekend with him. The following part of my narration of events will, no doubt, in the eyes of any reader, make me appear very naive and gullible. In my own defence I can only say that I was, as they say, in love. People, who are in love, it is well known, are not entirely rational. In addition I have to say that Rudi was a very persuasive, plausible man. During the course of the weekend, Rudi told me that the businessman whom he worked for "dabbled" in drugs supplying them to students, professional people and the like. Here again I will appear naive, gullible and stupid but as we were in Amsterdam I assumed he meant cannabis products. Now of course possession of soft drugs for personal use is not a crime in the city (and nor is it a crime in Spain.) Rudi asked me to deliver a package for him to a business acquaintance in Madrid. I did protest that that was supplying drugs. Don't worry he said the contents of the package were for his friend's personal use. Incredibly stupid as it may appear I did not ask what the contents of the package were, assuming it contained cannabis products. So it was that I flew back to Madrid in a state of considerable agitation and trepidation, fearfully imagining the scene at the airport as I was revealed as a drug smuggler. You can imagine my relief when I was waved through Customs. Not even the sniffer dog seemed to be must interested in me. I delivered the package to his business friend as instructed.

Rudi told me later that the package contained chocolates and that the entire charade had been a test of my reliability as a courier.

In this way I was sucked into that part of the criminal underworld populated by Jesus Maria Magdalena Peron and Rudi.

"Forgive me interrupting you but I take it this is the businessman for whom Rudi worked? You will give some description of this man and his activities?"

"Yes. He was from Peru and had come to live in Berlin as part of an extended family group. He completed his education in Berlin qualifying as a doctor and working in that profession and city for a number of years. When he reached 30 years of age he decided on a change of direction in life and came to seek his fortune in Amsterdam-if that is an appropriate phrase, given what I now know of his activities.

A few days ago in Barcelona a large consignment of cocaine was delivered by an American officer working for Jesus Peron to one of his agents there, a Consuela M.... It was then given into the custody of another agent of Jesus, a Vanessa S.... She, together with her policeman husband delivered it to a woman I had come to know through my studies and fieldwork. Her name is Maria de G... and the handover took place in the Ritz in Madrid.

I had no idea of the size of the consignment. We then drove to Versailles with the consignment in her Mercedes.

That is all I wish to place on record at this stage. To repeat, I had no idea at the time what the consignment contained or its size."

CHAPTER NINETEEN
Extract of a statement given to the police of Amsterdam by Captain Jan Van P..., ordinary member of The Dutch Reformed Church, on 25 May 2013.

My full name is Jan van P... and I hold the rank of Captain in the police of Amsterdam. I am 26 years of age.
Unusually for a policeman making a statement in an investigation I will allude briefly to some details of my antecedents for reasons which will soon become apparent.
I suppose I can say (modestly I hope) that I had been something of a "star" in my year at The Law School of Amsterdam. Add to that, a certain *panache* in the avocations of my youth, for example parachuting, and I, as they say, "came to the attention" of the Government agencies of The Netherlands. Those agencies decided that it might be best to place me, most promising material as I appeared to be, in the Amsterdam police to begin with. No point, after all, in a direct induction into the more exotic agencies of The Kingdom of The Netherlands at a very young and inexperienced age. I was obviously destined at some point to be on my way to employment with the governing agencies of the State.
Prior to my transfer to the government agencies, I spent the last two months or so of my police career in charge of a pleasant little police station (if there

be such a thing) on the fringes of The Vondel Park. The principal duties in the station appeared to consist of sharpening biros, reading the newspaper and occasionally arresting that abomination of modern life, namely professional footballers. One or two of this branch of Homo sapiens had purchased properties in the neighbourhood, said purchases being no doubt intended as intimation to their fellow man that they "had made it". That is as maybe but they were unable to refrain from their overindulgence in the liquids favoured by the God Bacchus after a match and sometimes had to be invited to stay with us at the police station in Marystraat.

In those halcyon days the only truly challenging circumstances facing me were the biannual visits of my irascible father-in-law from Scotland, a gentleman in his seventies. Most of us find the elderly exasperating and struggle to cope. I certainly did. He regarded all Amsterdam as his personal domain, ranging from The Concertgebouw to every Art Gallery from The Rijksmuseum to The Van Gogh and The Hermitage. He expected me to provide chauffeur driven transport wherever he went, said transport taking the form of a police car to take him wherever wanted to go. It was very annoying.

Just how many more times I wondered, would I have to endure this person from the outer reaches of The Roman Empire-a country which Hadrian had seen fit to enclose behind a wall? The worst aspect of his conduct was that he always arrived- and remained during his visit-in full Highland dress and bearing his bagpipes. To the outrage of his

daughter and me, he insisted on performing on the same. Exasperated one evening and fearful of complaints from the neighbours, my wife suggested that he take his Highland dress and bagpipes and perform on the same in front of The Royal Palace in Dam Square. He promptly did and returned with 78 Euros which the demented tourists had given him as a reward for his musical endeavours! I suppose that those who care for elderly parents with dementia may say that there is worse to befall the offspring of senior citizens but I doubt it.
The readers of this statement may wonder where this narration of events is leading. Let me explain. An incident occurred at the Marystraat police station which has led my superiors to question my fitness for high office.
I had arranged to meet with my father-in-law after the day's shift. The conclusion of my shift consisted of the interrogation of one of the few criminals who reside near the station. There is something intrinsically difficult about conducting an interrogation when one's father-in-law is playing the bagpipes outside the police station. The virtuoso performance of such musical masterpieces as "Hen's March to the Midden" and "Flower of Scotland" was justified, my father-in-law later argued on the grounds of it being a beautiful day thus reminding him of the Scottish Highlands at their best.
"For Christ's sake," the criminal under interrogation had complained, "can you not stop that old bastard making such a din?"
Tiresome though my father-in-law was, I took umbrage at this description of my father-in-law and

informed the criminal accordingly. By this time a crowd of spectators had gathered to enjoy the performance. I decided to confront my father-in-law and went outside to remonstrate with him.
"Will you stop making that infernal din?" I shouted above the noise of the bagpipes.
"The bagpipes are not an infernal din laddie," he replied in between puffing on his musical instrument.
Across the street on the balcony of a house overlooking the police station I noticed a man whom I now know to be Jesus Maria Magdalena Peron and some of his friends. He was wearing a red hat and clapping wildly.

(Note inserted in the margin by the senior officer in charge of the investigation: You couldn't make this up, could you? It's like the comic interlude in a Shakespearean drama- Utterly surreal!)

To continue with my statement, it is only after the mule Norma decided to make a statement that I became aware of what was taking place under our very noses in the Marystraat police station. It is a cause of deep embarrassment to me that a major drug smuggling ring could function within metres of the police station in which I worked for the last days of my police career. And yet, in my own defence, I am surely allowed to make the eminently reasonable point that all manner of illegalities might occur within any given radius of a police station and the occupants of said station remain unaware of them. The law does require evidence of wrong doing and we had none. Not a shred of evidence had come to light until the mule made her statement. It must be remembered that this gang consisted of foreigners and therefore, at least in relation to their criminal activities, kept matters close to their chest.

Having regard to the evidence which has now been ingathered and cross checking with my diary, I regret to say that the occupants of the house owned by Jesus Peron never came to the attention of me or my officers. The point has been made to me that surely I and/or my men must have noticed people living near the station who were obviously a foreign group. I have to point out that as in any major city of the world there are many people of foreign or mixed race. Mixed ethnicity in itself is not a reason for police interest. If it were we would no doubt be accused of being racist.

Lastly I have to say something about the husband of Vanessa S.... I can only record my profound disappointment that a colleague in whom so much trust was reposed saw fit to betray that trust in so flagrant a manner. I am well aware that he and his no less treacherous wife visited Spain for long weekends with a frequency that was almost indecent. However, at the time, I knew nothing of what they were up to and naturally assumed that she was visiting family in Spain.

In conclusion I wish to place on the record that I had no dealings with the other members of the drug smuggling ring. Their names and photographs meant nothing to me with the exception of the solitary occasion I saw Jesus Peron applauding my father-in-law's efforts on the bagpipes.

On reflection perhaps I will be allowed to amend that last remark. In April 2013 I attended the opening of the Rijksmuseum. It was a state occasion attended by many distinguished people. There was a firework display. My father-in-law was quite overwhelmed by the occasion. He enthused about the orange fireworks and it was only with great difficult that I restrained him from once more giving all who would listen to him a stirring bagpipe medley. I had a glimpse of Vanessa S... in the crowd with her husband and a man I now know to be Rudi. There was no contact with him that day. However, "for my sins", I was sent to note a statement from him after his arrest and an indication from that he was willing to cooperate in exchange for a lighter sentence.

My superiors have indicated that I am to be transferred to other duties forthwith and after a period of further assessment a decision taken on my future.

(Note inserted in the margin by the senior investigating officer:-

"Perhaps this officer's superiors will consider having him re-employed as a tram driver on the Number Two Line! I see little other use for him.")

CHAPTER TWENTY
Santa Maria hotel, Bay of Naples, on 11 May 2013

URGENT SECURE EMAIL (I hope) for the State Prosecutor of The Kingdom of The Netherlands from the investigating officer-in-charge in the Jesus Peron case.

Sir,
I have just attended at the base headquarters of the American Sixth Fleet which, as you know, is in Naples.
I find it difficult (as do many policemen and lawyers) to conceal my contempt for the armed services and the security services of any country. It is their boundless capacity for seeking to evade their responsibility for crimes that so distresses me. While we, in civilian life accept full responsibility for any of our actions which are deemed to be criminal, these cowards invoke their tedious Mantra of "national security" or any one of many other nebulous, meaningless phrases designed to cover up their own corruption and wrong doing.
As instructed I was in possession of a warrant for the arrest of Lieutenant Commander Brad Alaska of the Sixth Fleet in respect of the illegal importation of twenty-five kilograms of pure cocaine three days ago in Barcelona and when I boarded the aircraft carrier in the Bay of Naples I

was met by an admiral who conveyed me to his private apartments. I explained that I was in possession of a warrant for the arrest of Alaska. Surprise, surprise! The admiral said that he would, of course, cooperate with the lawful authorities of any democratic nation but humbly requested that I return forty-eight hours later when he would have had the benefit of legal advice of the State Department in Foggy Bottom, Washington! Words fail me!

He then handed me a "redacted" statement from the Lieutenant Commander bearing to be a "full and frank" admission of guilt.

Sir, you will be well aware of the practice of the military and security services of any country in providing "redacted" statements. By said means, these morons (forgive me, I have been sorely tried in the last hour or two) hope to escape punishment (and embarrassment) to their own governments for anything from war crimes, crimes against humanity and plain ordinary torture.

Sir, the American Navy and all other armed services are bound by The Joint Forces Act and are prohibited from carrying out any act which is illegal under American law or that of the host country. It is my belief that the American Navy will seek to spirit Lieutenant Commander Alaska out of Italy and to somewhere beyond the jurisdiction of The Kingdom of The Netherlands or her allies.

I therefore request that urgent contact be had with NATO headquarters in Brussels and the government of the United States for assistance in the arrest of what is, after all, a man accused of major drug a crime in respect of whom there is an abundance of evidence and a lawful warrant.

CHAPTER TWENTY ONE
Amsterdam central criminal court, 13 September 2013
Evidence of the mule, Norma.

Piet Mondrian (hereinafter PM): Do you mind if I call you Norma?
Norma (hereinafter N): As you please.
PM: Thank you. My name as you have gathered is Piet Mondrian. My parents had artistic ambitions for me but I rather let them down and became a lawyer instead. Now Norma, you have told the court that you do not have your troubles to seek in life. You have told the court that you have tertiary syphilis, Aids and concomitant health problems as a result of which your life expectancy is not great. Is that all correct?
N: Yes.
PM: And is it also correct that you are currently serving a four-year prison term for diamond smuggling?
N: Yes.
PM: Nonetheless I have a duty to the State to canvass certain matters with you. Do you understand?
N: Yes.
PM: Do you accept that your conduct has not only brought disgrace upon yourself and your family but it also precipitated a turbulent period in this country's domestic politics?
N: Yes, I accept that.
PM: You were born into wealth and privilege?
N: Yes.

PM: What is your understanding of how your family came to acquire such influence?

N: My grandfather acquired a reputation as something of a war hero by providing information to the Allies and especially the British.

PM: Do you know what kind of information he provided to them?

N: Anything from troop movements to which windmills were working. In my opinion, his reputation as a war hero was ill-deserved. He was simply trying to save his own skin after serving, as many Dutch did, in the SS. However his so-called heroic conduct won him the support of the British. After the war he prospered as a lawyer. In due course, my father took over the firm and my grandfather's impressive list of contacts. You have to understand that those with the right social background and wartime intelligence service seemed to either know everyone who "mattered" in every country. I have met many of these people and many are just worthless human flotsam.

PM: In the days of your youth and before the ravages of illness, you were considered something of a beauty?

N: Yes.

PM: To canvass matters shortly, what happened to you?

N: Once upon a time I saw someone to whom I was really attracted.

PM: And was there a romance?

N: No. I never even went out with him. My parents made enquiries and decided he was from the wrong background, wholly unsuitable.

PM: How so?

N: He and his family had no money. My father and his cronies in the security services then proceeded to make his life a living hell. They bugged his house and subjected him to a degree of surveillance that was tantamount to torture.
PM: So how did you take this?
N: Not well. I was advised "to play the field".
PM: And did you?
N: Yes but I cannot really blame my parents for what I did. I had a string of lovers and once even slept with the young man's best friend. Looking back on it, I have to say that I was a single child and from very early years encouraged by my parents and their appalling friends that I was somehow such a privileged and beautiful child that there was no requirement for me to observe the normal rules of civilised conduct. In short I was spoiled and did exactly as I pleased.
PM: Did you follow in the family tradition and practice law?
N: No, I could not abide legal practice. I was offered a management post in the Post Office.
PM: Some may wonder why you took such employment.
N: It was just a question of waiting for the "right man" to appear.
PM: A man your parents approved of?
N: Yes.
PM: And did this beau ever appear?
N: No.
PM: You were a wealthy young woman were you not?
N: Yes but I squandered my inheritance in two or more years.

PM: And then the problems began?
N: Yes. It all seemed to happen at once. Shortly after I learned I had venereal disease and ran out of money I encountered Jesus and his sidekick Rudi.
PM: Where did you encounter them?
N: On tram number two. I was on my way to The Concertgebouw and had taken the tram because I wanted to drink at the interval. I can't remember how the conversation started but they were going to the concert too and before I knew where I was I had joined them for the evening. They made for amusing company.
PM: When did you realise that they were drug dealers?
N: It wasn't long before I realised they were dealers. The picture they painted was that they only bought for and dealt to friends and at cost price. They placed great emphasis on that and the fact that they only dealt in soft drugs. Before long I was running "errands" for them.
PM: Where to?
N: Here in the city and to Rotterdam and elsewhere.
PM: Did you not suspect that far from delivering soft drugs to their friends you were carrying Class A drugs?
N: Yes, of course but the money was good and I needed the money.
PM: Typically what were you paid?
N: It depended on the "errand". There were occasions when I had to make what they called "special" deliveries...
PM: ...and you rightly guessed that you were being asked to carry and deliver Class A drugs?

N: Yes.
PM: You did not work for them over a lengthy period of time?
N: That is correct but I think it fair to say that I acquired quite a knowledge of their activities in that period.
PM: We shall come to that in a moment. Was it about this time that you, as it were, became involved in the diamond trade?
N: Yes.
PM: Tells us about that.
N: I knew from my wealthy and extremely stupid friends that there was much money to be made from smuggling uncut diamonds into the country.
PM: To take matters in short compass, you did so but were caught at Schipol airport?
N: Yes.
PM: Did Jesus Peron have anything to do with diamond smuggling?
N: No.
PM: After your apprehension in connection with the illegal movement of diamonds your parents made frantic efforts on your behalf to have the charges dropped?
N: Yes.
PM: Again, to take matters in short compass, your father used or attempted to use his extensive network of contacts both here and in the United States in order to free you?
N: Yes.
PM: In this country he made approaches to the former Prime Minister, Wolfgang Amadeus Van der Heath and the head of the Dutch security services, Vice Admiral Louis le Batard?

N: Yes. I did not approve.
PM: Oh, why so?
N: Both men were notorious homosexuals with particular interest in homosexual Amsterdam policemen...
PM: May I stop you there? Again to take matters in short compass, the attempts made on your behalf by the former prime minister and the former head of the security services became public knowledge and both men were forced to resign?
N: Yes.
PM: The attempt by your father to secure the assistance of the President of The United States on your behalf was rebuffed; you stood trial and were convicted?
N: Yes.
PM: Now may we turn to what you knew of the activities of Jesus Peron beyond the borders of The Netherlands both in Germany and Spain?
N: As you know my activities as a courier were largely confined to The Netherlands but Jesus would sometimes talk about his operations in both countries.
PM: Some people might find it strange that a man who was engaged in international drug smuggling would confide or impart information to a mere mule.
N: I think Jesus liked me. I think it had something to do with his two middle Christian names...
PM: What do you mean?
N: He saw me as a "fallen woman". He was certainly careless and ill-advised in disclosing such matters to me.

PM: Plainly he did not consider that one day you would be caught for the illegal movement of diamonds and then betray him and his organisation to the authorities?

N: Obviously not. I suppose the term "Judas" must now be added to the invective already heaped on my head...

PM: What other invective?

N: Cow, slut, whore...et cetera.

PM: Describe what you knew of the German operations.

N: I can't in any detail. I can only relate what Jesus let slip. He had an extensive network in Germany and ran many mules through the country. Most travelled up from the well-known routes from the Middle East and into Romania, Hungary and Austria and then crossed the German border via the Bodensee or even through Switzerland into Germany. Once in the country the drugs were brought north either through the railway hub in Koblenz or occasionally by road. I must say Jesus favoured the railways. He had a thing about them.

PM: Describe the Spanish network.

N: I know a lot about that. Jesus and Rudi were very proud-if that is the word-of their Spanish agents. There were two main centres of activity-Madrid and Barcelona. In Barcelona a girl Rudi had recruited by the name of Consuela M... She was the main agent.

PM: Describe what she did on behalf of the organisation run by Jesus Peron.

N: She was based in Barcelona and the main focal point for any drug consignments originating in Morocco or the Costas. Assuming the consignment

was adjudged to be of relatively low financial value a courier or mule would be despatched from Amsterdam by plane, the drugs uplifted and then driven back to the north. If the consignment was adjudged to be of high value, Jesus would take greater precautions and would despatch one of his more trusted operatives from Amsterdam, a Vanessa S... and her husband.
PM: Describe this girl and her husband please.
N: As the name suggests, she was Spanish-from Madrid. She had, would you believe, a good law degree from the University of Madrid but had been unable to find work there due to a combination of the then prevailing economic situation and, coming from a poor background, her family knew no one to pull strings on her behalf. She ended up in Amsterdam looking for work. She managed to find work at the Cafe des Amis in Marystraat...
PM: Across the road from a residence owned by Jesus Peron?
N: Correct. There is a police station just opposite the Cafe des Amis, patronised by policemen on coffee or lunch breaks. She started going out with one of them and subsequently married him.
PM: And do you seriously suggest that this policeman, along with his wife, from time to time flew to Barcelona, there to uplift large drug consignments.
N: I do and there is no suggestion about it. I know for a fact that he did although I would say that he was distant from the detail of any given operation.
PM: How so?
N: You must understand that many people today are hard up for money...

PM: I do live in this world.
N: Sorry. Look Rudi was screwing Vanessa but she and her husband were hard up. Her husband did not enquire too deeply into the precise nature of her relationship with Rudi or the quantities and type of drugs that were being smuggled. When a large consignment arrived in Barcelona by whatever means, it was Consuela M... who took possession of it in the first instance. Thereafter and once everyone was satisfied that she was not being tailed, it would be handed over to Vanessa somewhere in the city-usually at the Sagrada Familia...
PM: Jesus Peron was of a religious bent?
N: I'll deal with that matter later if I may.
PM: Please continue.
N: Vanessa and her husband would then take the consignment to Madrid by hired car.
PM: Surely such a method of conveyance was not without its dangers?
N: All methods of conveyance have inherent dangers. If stopped for say some minor traffic offence, Vanessa's husband's Amsterdam police identification always worked.
PM: Once they and the consignment arrived in Madrid, what then?
N: Jesus was very proud-if that is the word-of his acquaintanceship with a Madrid society lady whose name is Maria de G.... Her family owned a large estate outside Toledo and it was to there that the large consignments were usually taken. Maria de G... was friendly with a girl from the Madrid Vetenery School. Her name was Agnes le Bailey. She was in the process of completing her studies. Rudi had recruited her. Her parents had a practice

in Versailles and lived on a small estate outside the town.

PM: In May this year you learned of a large consignment arriving in Barcelona?

N: Yes."

PM: "Please tell the court what you learned about the arrival of this large consignment and in as much detail as you recall.

N: In early May I had just returned from a routine mission to Rotterdam and taken Tram Number Two to Marystraat to report to Rudi...

PM: You did not go to the residence maintained By Jesus Peron?

N: No. Visits to the house were strictly controlled and rare. Cafe des Amis was the branch office, so to speak. I must confess to a certain childish thrill sitting outside Cafe des Amis sipping a coffee or a glass of wine just two or three metres from the police station and reporting on my latest mule activity. Adding to my childish thrill was the knowledge that one of Jesus' most trusted operatives not only worked the cafe but also that her husband occasionally worked out of the Marystraat station and together with his wife smuggled some of the largest drug consignments into this country. I must confess that on such occasions I would often wave to policemen entering or leaving the station or those working within...

PM: I think our friends in psychology term such conduct "breaking the rules"?

N: Fuck psychologists.

JUDGE: Remember you are in a court of law. Moderate your language or I shall add to the length of the sentence you are serving.
N: I apologise, Sir.
JUDGE: Continue with your evidence.
N: Rudi was pleased with the results of my trip to Rotterdam and bought me a glass of my favourite red wine. I noticed that he appeared to be nervous and I asked what was troubling me. He said that knowledge could be a dangerous thing and that it would be best if I did not know. First rule in drug smuggling and espionage, I believe he said.
PM: But he did eventually tell you what was troubling him.
N: Yes, he did. We all make mistakes I suppose...
PM: A fatal error on his part as subsequent events has demonstrated?
N: Yes, it certainly was. I wish he hadn't told me. I was about to fly to South Africa to pick up the diamonds. As you know, I was apprehended at Schipol on my return.
PM: So what information did Rudi eventually disclose to you?
N: In his state of nervous anxiety he eventually confided in me. He did so, so he said, because he knew that Jesus trusted me.
PM: Information which after your arrest you disclosed to the authorities in the hope and expectation of receiving a lighter sentence in respect of your foray into the diamond business and in the hope that you yourself would escape charges in respect of your activities as a mule?

N: Yes. Rudi told me that within the next few days an unusually large consignment of drugs would be brought to Barcelona...
PM: Did Rudi tell you who and by what means this consignment would be brought to Barcelona?
N: Yes, he did. Rudi told me that recently Jesus had achieved something of a spectacular coup in the field of recruitment of drug mules.
PM: And who was this "spectacular coup"?
N: An American naval officer who worked as a drug liaison officer. This posting allowed this person to travel freely between any countries in the world-all without "let or hindrance" as they say in diplomatic terms...
PM: Did Rudi give you the name of this officer and how Jesus had secured his services?
N: No, neither.
PM: Pray, continue.
N: Rudi was worried. It all seemed too good to be true and if it is too good to be true...
PM: ...then it cannot be true?
N: Exactly. However Jesus was for once in a state of some agitation and quite in contrast to his usual sangfroid which was legendary. For once he and Rudi were planning to fly down to Barcelona there to superintend the operation from a distance.
PM: What can you tell us about the detail of the operation?
N: Much the same for the delivery of any other major drug consignment in Barcelona. Consuela M... would take possession of the consignment and, once everyone was satisfied that neither she nor the officer were the subject of surveillance surrender

custody of the consignment to Vanessa S... and her husband at...
PM: ...The Sagrada Familia?
N: Just so.
PM: Did you have any opinion on the forthcoming operation or offer any words of counsel?
N: No. Firstly it was not my place so to do and secondly I was preoccupied with my imminent trip to South Africa.
PM: So, to round matters off, Rudi went off to Barcelona and you to South Africa?
N: Yes.
PM: Thank you for your evidence which, I do realise must have been difficult for you to give. There is one last matter. Jesus was obviously a major offender against the laws prohibiting the smuggling and distribution of drugs. That said, did he have any other agendas? Beyond making as much money as possible, that is.
N: I think he did. I think there was a political agenda.
PM: A political agenda? What political agenda?
N: It was all very nebulous and inchoate. And it was complicated. You must understand what motivated Jesus more than anything. He was outraged by the treatment of his family-of peasant stock-in his native country. On the one hand, the government-under American pressure-professed to deplore drugs. And this was in a country and culture where drugs, at least for personal use, had been tolerated for centuries. On the other hand, he knew from history that the Americans during the long years of "The Pax America"-now thankfully coming to an end as the United States goes into

terminal decline-had long used and manipulated drugs to advance whatever political cause they favoured and this in any country in the world. If Jesus had a political agenda it was this: he wanted to make as much money from drugs as he could and especially at the expense of any American backed groups and then return to his native country as a very rich man there to acquire a political base and power but by legitimate means. There to advance the condition and well-being of his people and the peoples of South America generally.

PM: And to this end he gave up the prospect of a brilliant career in medicine?

N: So did Che. Once upon a time we had so-called Communism and so-called democracy. The latter purported to believe in Christ and the former had, what one German commentator called "a "black" pope, an ideologue called Suslov. You could say that Jesus Peron intended to be a "black" saviour for people in his native land and those of all South American people.

PM: Not sure I understood that but let me tell you that I occasionally travel on Tram Number Two myself when I go to visit my son, daughter-in-law and grandson. In the light of your evidence about the divinity and political sophistication of those who use Tram Number Two, I promise I shall look upon my fellow passengers with new respect and awe.

(Note: laughter in court.)

CHAPTER TWENTY TWO
Evidence of Rudi, the German drug dealer, Amsterdam central criminal court, 14 September 2013

PM: Rudi, thank you for giving evidence today and what appears to be a truthful account of your role in matters. There are however two episodes you have not referred to and which I wish to canvass with you.
Firstly I wish to take from you an account of your visit to Morocco earlier this year and the second episode relates to the extent to which Jesus Peron gained entree into Amsterdam society. The first matter, I believe, demonstrates the risks run by mules and the second demonstrates the danger to a society in too readily accepting a person in their midst merely on the grounds that they appear to have an inordinate amount of money.
Please describe your visit to Morocco to the court.
R: Jesus had secured 300,000 Euro's worth of hashish oil from a contact in Morocco and there remained the little matter of bringing it back to Europe.
PM: And were you selected for the task?
R: Yes.
PM: You must have less than overjoyed about being selected for so dangerous a task?
R: Precisely. You can never be too careful these days-even in Morocco. It is no longer the free and easy drug trading paradise it was in the 1960s, 1970s and 80s. Western governments (hypocritical

to the last) have forced the Moroccans to crack down on the drug trade. No pun is intended.
PM: How did Jesus expect you bring such a bulky consignment into Europe?
R: I flew into Agadir in Morocco as a tourist on a week's holiday. In the middle of the week I had taken a tourist bus trip from Agadir to Marrakesh. On the way back we stopped-as we had on the outward journey-at a garage in the middle of nowhere. It was there that I met Jesus' contact and took possession of a Volkswagen caravanette from him. In it was the consignment of hashish oil.
PM: What did the man have to say for himself?
R: Very little. He was more concerned with the progress of a football match which was on television in the cafe adjoining the garage. I should explain that Morocco was playing Mozambique. It was a qualifying match for the world cup. The local Moroccans were hugely excited and animated by the match and amid much noisy exhortation of their players I don't think anyone paid us any attention which was probably the idea behind meeting Jesus' contact there and at the time the match was on.
PM: Handover of the VW caravanette with its consignment of hashish oil complete what next?
R: I followed the tourist bus back to Agadir...
PM: One moment, did the tourist guide on the bus you had been travelling on have anything to say about you completing your trip in a vehicle other than that which had conveyed you to Marrakesh and, thus far, back in the direction of Agadir?
R: No. 50 Euros is usually enough to buy any man's silence in Morocco.

PM: Where did you go once back in Agadir?
R: The docks. I had arranged passage to Spain on a cargo ship bound for Barcelona.
PM: And once in Barcelona what then?
R: Barcelona, as all Spanish cities or, for that matter, cities anywhere in the world, has its share of corrupt officials. Customs in Barcelona scarcely looked at the road I was on.
PM: Where did you after Barcelona?
R: North over the Pyrenees and into France. That was the most dangerous phase of the whole operation. To be stopped for even a minor road traffic infringement could have spelled disaster.
PM: Where exactly in the VW caravanette was the hashish oil?
R: In petrol canisters. Petrol stinks and so does hashish oil. That's the reason it was stashed in petrol canisters.
PM: Did you reach The Netherlands without incident?
R: Yes, Thank God.
PM: May I now turn to the entree into Amsterdam society that Jesus Peron was beginning to develop as a result of his...how can I put?...his increasing prosperity.
R: Certainly. While Jesus had his residence in Marystraat, he was most proud of one of his other abodes.
PM: And what was this abode?
R: Jesus kept a houseboat on the Herren Gracht. A number of points require attention. Firstly, anyone who knows anything about Amsterdam should know that it is almost impossible to obtain a new permit for a houseboat especially on the grander

canals. The City Council has long since set its face against the grant of new permits...
PM: Did Peron bribe city officials?
R: I have no evidence of that. To use police jargon his modus operandi was to make lavish contributions to well-known charities in the city and The Netherlands generally. Within a relatively short space of time he found himself invited to many functions and rubbing shoulders, as they say, with the so-called "great and good". Now, as you may know, wealthy people are encouraged by psychologists to adopt a charity in order to remain "grounded". With Jesus his "charity" work was rather a means of take-off than any desire to remain "grounded". Do remember that in addition Jesus could exude charm, had a way with words and a natural charm which won him friends easily. The next point to notice is that with the money Jesus was making from his nefarious activities he could have well afforded to buy one of the more splendid residences on the Herren Gracht...
PM: Why didn't he?
R: He is an astute man. While it is true to say that many of the former grand residences have been bought as company and banking headquarters, there are quite a number still in private hands. Jesus reckoned that if he purchased a grand residence he would almost certainly come to the attention of government agencies and thus become the subject of most unwelcome surveillance. It would be a step too far. Better by far, he reasoned to select the houseboat option where, with any luck, he would be regarded simply as a vulgar *parvenu* and *arriviste* unworthy of close examination.

PM: So what went on at the houseboat?
R: He entertained and on a lavish scale. It was a splendid boat with seven apartments and a garden roof upon which Jesus discretely grew best quality cannabis plants more as a devil-may-care gesture as opposed to industrial production.
PM: How and who did he entertain?
R: Just about everyone who was anyone in the city. Jesus was particularly adept in throwing expensive soirees for the hoi polloi. These included the provision of musical ensembles. For once there was no wind pipe band. The ensembles played only a classical repertoire and Jesus was always a sober suited gentleman on these occasions. For his friends in the Art world his latest acquisitions were always on display to the envy of his acquaintances at The Hermitage and the Van Gogh.
PM: Did Jesus not worry about the security of his possessions and indeed his person?
R: No. Jesus did not feel unprotected there. A very large Columbian who wore a solid gold Crucifix around his neck and had a matching gold Glock pistol stuffed down his trousers was never far away. Such a measure deters most men.
PM: Anything you would like to add?
R: No. I think I have painted a vivid picture.
PM: Thank you for giving evidence.

CHAPTER TWENTY THREE
Evidence of Jesus Maria Magdalena Peron, Amsterdam central criminal court, 16 September 2013

PM: Your full name is Jesus Maria Magdalena Peron?
JP: That is correct.
PM: And you are 33 years of age having been born on 3rd March 1980 in Peru?
JP: That is also correct.
PM: You have in the course of these proceedings dismissed your legal counsel and tendered pleas of guilty to the charges against you?
JP: Yes, that is correct.
PM: That said, you have asked the court to hear you in mitigation and on oath and the court has agreed?
JP: Yes, I would like to give the court the circumstances surrounding the crimes in respect of which I have tendered pleas of guilty.
PM: Very well. Please say what you want to say. I may occasionally interrupt if I think that anything you say requires clarification.
JP: I begin my evidence dealing with the name given to me by my parents when I emerged into this world. There is nothing unusual about it in the Spanish world. Jesus is a common given name and nor is there anything untoward about the two middle names. I shall return to this matter shortly.

I was born in a small farming community outside the city of Concepcion. When I say farming community perhaps it would be more accurate to describe it a community of small holdings. Life was hard: it was subsistence farming. Peasant stock in the land of my birth see nothing unusual in the use of what is called "drugs" in the West as a means of escaping the hardship of their daily life and/or a means of supplementing their income. By no stretch of the imagination could such economic activity be equated with the nefarious activities of international drug cartels. Such activity was simply part of their culture.

Life for the peasants is hard beyond measure in fact. They are squeezed incessantly in a nut cracker of rapacious landlords charging exorbitant rents and a government which, intermittently, is anxious to please the Americans and international economic agencies by stamping out any "extra-curricular" economic activity among the peasants...

PM: Did you ever take drugs in childhood or early adolescent years?

JP: Rarely. It was akin to young people in Europe being given their first glass of wine by indulgent or incautious parents. May I continue?

PM: Of course.

JP: By the time I was nine years old, that is in 1989, my family and extended family which is rather large was in desperate circumstances. As a group they decided to leave the country and seek to prosper elsewhere. Some in fact had already left and gone to seek work and a better life in places as diverse as Cuba and Germany. My parents decided to try to make a go of things in Germany. They were fortunate to secure entry in 1990. They were hugely assisted by my uncle who was already in Berlin and prepared to offer them accommodation. Further, he told the authorities that he had jobs for them which was something of a distortion of the truth. However, to cut a long story short, they were allowed in. I think they were aided by the fact that central Berlin in those days was chaos and a large building site. Rules and regulations were not always closely followed.

PM: Presumably you for your part were kept busy by the need to learn German and attend school rather than the broader economic situation which your parents were absorbed by?

JP: Yes. And it was at school that I quickly learned how much amusement my name caused in the West. It was very hurtful. I was little more than a child and found the constant harassment difficult to cope with. I cannot remember exactly when I found a defence mechanism to cope with the situation.

PM: The method you chose to deal with a very hurtful situation was to treat it as a joke and later to portray phases or episodes in your life by drawing analogies to episodes in the life of The Saviour?

JP: Yes.

JP: We have heard evidence in court about how you likened a drug dealing episode you were involved in at the age of fourteen outside The Kaiser Wilhelm Church in Berlin as similar to the precocity shown by The Saviour at the same age conversing with wise men of the temple. Is that true?

JP: Yes but it was neither a good analogy nor very funny but at fourteen, you say and do stupid things.
PM: Where did you get the drugs from?
JP: Through one of my brothers who had remained behind in my native land.
PM: What? Sent through the post?
JP: Of course not, that would be far too dangerous.
PM: How then?
JP: I have given evidence that my family was scattered to the four winds. Several went to Cuba. There a major world power has a large presence...
PM: I take it you mean the Chinese?
JP: Yes.
PM: You are not suggesting that Chinese officials connived at drug smuggling?
JP: Of course not. That means the death sentence. What I am saying is that individual Chinese are, like most people, never averse to making a little extra money. The Chinese also have a presence in my native land.
PM: And in later life once you had settled in Amsterdam you turned once more to Chinese people to assist with your smuggling activities?
JP: Yes, they were a big source but by no means the only source.
PM: Can you tell the court how drugs were smuggled from your native land to Cuba?
JP: No. To this day I have no idea how they did it and it is never a good idea to enquire too deeply into matters where the Chinese are concerned. They have little time for anyone who is not of their own family and that means being Chinese. All I do know is that once anything I asked for was delivered to Cuba I could let out a sigh of relief.

No-one dares to stop large Chinese ships without good reason.
PM: Once across the Atlantic the drugs would then have to be delivered to you?
JP: Sometimes almost to the doorstep. I had one Chinese contact here and, if I may, will describe the nature of that contact later.
PM: Very well. Please continue.
JP: The consignments got larger and larger. I was also dealing with suppliers from the normal sources for European dealers: from the Middle East through Romania, Bulgaria and The Czech Republic through Hungary and Austria and Switzerland and into Germany and from Morocco and other African countries into Spain where the main collection points I set up were in Barcelona and Madrid...
PM: It might be helpful if in the dichotomy of activity you have adumbrated, you begin with a description of your Spanish network and then describe the German network...
JP: I'm not sure I know what you mean...
JUDGE: Yes, Mr Mondrian, not all of us have acquired your level of erudition. And surely it should be trichotomy anyway given the participation of Chinese nationals? Please use plain language please.
PM: Certainly. Describe the set-up in Spain please.
JP: The Spanish network was the network I valued most-for personal reasons.
PM: Why was that?
JP: It must sound trite but I was in love with one of them.
PM: Maria de G...?

JP: Yes. I presume one of your investigators informed you.
PM: Where did you meet her?
JP: In Madrid at an upmarket tango establishment.
PM: She had certain advantages to your organisation?
JP: I will not deny it. She is well-known in Madrid society...
PM: ...and well-off?
JP: Not sure I understand the question. I am well-off given the millions I have gathered through legal and illegal activities.
PM: How was she useful to your organisation?
JP: Her family had an estate outside Toledo and it was sometimes convenient and very safe to take consignments there. In addition one of the girls Rudi had recruited-Agnes Le B...- who was studying in Madrid did work experience on the estate. Agnes' family lived in Versailles and consignments could be moved safely from Madrid to Versailles by both ladies. It was after all unlikely that someone of Maria de G...'s standing would be stopped by the authorities in either country.
PM: Please tell the court about the other agents you had Spain.
JP: Rudi had recruited two other girls...
PM: Rudi something of a ladies' man?
JP: I wouldn't say so. Bit like the rest of us-picked up anything in a skirt who'd have him.
PM: Please continue.
JP: The other two girls were Consuela M... in Barcelona and Vanessa S... in Amsterdam. Consuela was an American citizen but had a South American mother and a father who was American

but of Spanish descent. She hated him. He was one of those military types. So far as I could gather she ended up marrying some guy she didn't love-never a good idea. All consignments from Morocco and the Costas were filtered through her.
PM: And the other girl? What did she do?
JP: Vanessa was Spanish and from Madrid. As you probably know she had a good law degree but couldn't find work and went to Amsterdam where she had a girl-friend who could put her up while she looked for work. She eventually found a job in the Cafe des Amis...
PM: All roads seem to lead to the Cafe des Amis.
JP: Not quite but we used it almost as a branch office. She met a policeman from the nearby station and married him. Again in her case as with Consuela I don't think it was the romance of the century. Rudi started screwing her and recruited her. I think her husband turned a blind eye to that and her work for us.
PM: The money was good?
JP: Yes. And for the larger consignments it was expedient to send both Vanessa and her husband to Barcelona and drive the goods back north. Her husband's police badge came in handy if they were ever stopped by police.
PM: Can you tell the court about the last transaction in Barcelona before your apprehension?
JP: Certainly. An American naval officer who served as a liaison officer between the various drug agencies was the mule who brought the stuff in...
PM: Yes, tell us how you recruited him.
JP: Maria had met him at some soiree at the American embassy in Madrid. She got talking to

him and had a long conversation with him. It was apparent to her that he fancied her and after one glass of wine too many said that he was not looking forward to his next posting. This was to Washington and he was rather worried about finding the money for the sort of residence he was expected to maintain. Over a period of weeks Maria got to know him and reeled him in. He was something of a dream from the point of view of my organisation. Because of his position he was able to travel to all countries almost without challenge.

PM: So how was the operation planned?

JP: The usual procedure was followed for receiving a large consignment. Consuela met the target, swept the goods for any electronic devices and then took a run around Barcelona for a few hours with a view to ascertaining whether she was being tailed. She wasn't and then rendezvoused with Vanessa and her husband at the Sagrada. They had hired a camping van and drove north. They arrived back in Amsterdam and then it started...

PM: The mule Norma was stopped at Schipol airport in possession of diamonds?

JP: Yes and as you know the police in several countries moved quickly. Vanessa and her husband managed to escape into Germany but were quickly apprehended.

PM: What do you want to say about the mule Norma?

JP: I should have listened to Rudi. He was right about her. She could not be trusted and betrayed us all. It was the English writer Alan Bennett, wasn't it, who remarked that people are prisoners of their own lives?

PM: I don't know.
JP: The prison library is well-stocked. You should try it sometime...
(Note: Laughter in court.)
PM: I shall bear your advice in mind should I ever end up resident there.
JP: A girl like Norma the mule is totally unable to act independently of her class and background. She depends on them for economic wellbeing and social approval. In the end that is all that matters to girls like that.
PM: I understand from her evidence that you and Rudi met her on Tram Number Two en route to a concert at the Concertgebouw?
JP: Yeah, that's right. She had taken the tram because she wanted to drink during the interval and I took the tram with Rudi because I couldn't be bothered digging the Maserati out of the garage for such a short trip. We spend the evening and concert in her company. Over a period of weeks we got to know her.
PM: To take matters in short compass you liked her and Rudi had his reservations?
JP: That's right. Rudi had a dim view of women which he largely kept to himself. His main point, as I have said, is that that kind of girl was potentially real trouble. She owed loyalty to the background she came from and would betray us at the drop of a hat.
PM: You took a different view?
JP: Yes. More fool me. Rudi got it right.
PM: Why did you decide to recruit her?
JP: This will make me look very stupid. She was attractive although not my colour scheme...

PM: I understand you like your women to be Spanish or at worst Italian?
JP: That I have to admit. However it soon emerged that she was a fallen woman in more ways than one. I felt sorry for her. More fool me. At the start I got her to run minor errands for the organisation and later allowed her to carry larger consignments.
PM: Then she betrayed all of you after her arrest at Schipol airport by reason of her possession of a large number of uncut diamonds?
JP: Yes.
PM: What was the first intimation you had of real trouble for you and your organisation?
JP: Rudi got a phone call on his mobile from her. She told him that she was in custody at the airport. It was too late to do much about it or anything. I tried to alert as many of my people as I could.
PM: Perhaps we can now turn to the German network?
JUDGE: Before you do Mr Mondrian. I am rather hungry. Can we adjourn till the afternoon?

PM: Senor Peron, I trust you had a satisfactory lunch at the expense of the tax payer.
JP: I've eaten in better establishments.
PM: Tell us about the German network, please.
JP: My role was a supervisory one. While I have German citizenship, Rudi is the real deal as it were, being from Rudesheim. The Rhine was an absolutely key strategic artery for us...
PM: ...As it has been throughout the centuries?
JP: Precisely. The Rhine is a key strategic artery what with its river traffic, trains running north to south and nearby autobahns doing the same. I

pretty much let Rudi get on with things. He knew the Rhine gorge and transportation systems like the back of his hand. As I got richer I was well able to afford to buy a powerful motor cruiser which I kept berthed near Cologne. If large consignments were on the move the boat was useful back-up if any of the mules got into trouble.
PM: Where did the drug consignments originate?
JP: The Middle East mainly. The usual routes are through Romania, Hungary, Albania and the Czech Republic and then through Austria or Switzerland into Germany and then on to Koblenz where there is a railway hub and access to the nearby autobahns...
PM: I understand that you are an admirer of German railways?
JP: I suppose I am. In any event there was never a single occasion when the boat was required to rescue a mule. Rudi was good at his job. We usually ended up in the boat at Koblenz admiring the "German Corner". Please don't make too much of that in my evidence. I just thought that Kaiser Bill, whose statue is there must have been the original "macho man" in Germany. My primary cultural orientation is the Spanish World and I can surely be forgiven my occasional frivolous moments.
PM: Can we now return to what I will term "religious" matters for the moment?
JP: I thought you might get round to that sooner or later.
PM: Quite so. You have already told us how you suffered in schooldays in Berlin by reason of your name, that is, Jesus Maria Magdalena Peron?
JP: Yes I did not enjoy those days.

PM: And your selected defence mechanism was that of humour? Perhaps some people would call it "black" humour?
JP: Yes.
PM: As your drug dealing activities enriched you, a former church in Amsterdam was purchased by you as office premises?
JP: It the former Church of the Doubting Thomas. The premises were on the Prinzen Gracht. You and the court will be aware that with the decline in the practice of religion and consequent decline in congregations, churches of various denominations have in recent years been sold off and turned into private residences or even restaurants and pubs.
PM: I think that is within the knowledge of the court. In my own home town there is bar which used to be the basement of a church. It is now called "Heavens Above Down Below"...
(Note: laughter in court.)
JP: Any change in the use of a building as a church is accompanied by a religious service of deconsecrating the building. Thus the building is no longer a sacred place of worship and no offence can be taken by anyone to the new purpose to which the building is put.
PM: And what use did you put the former Church of The Doubting Thomas?
JP: It became the Global Headquarters for The International Corporation for Fair Trade in Medical Products, that is, our drug-trafficking HQ.
(Note: laughter in court.)
PM: A condition of sale of the Church to you was that the edifice was to remain as it was?

JP: That is correct and I left most of the interior as it was too. It seemed a shame to destroy the interior. That said, the premises had to be made fit for purpose.
PM: And what did that entail?
JP: We had to move desks and chairs and of course the ubiquitous computers.
PM: The court has heard that the High Altar became a place to put flat screen computers on.
JP: That's right. It was also a place to hold meetings.
PM: The court has heard that the innermost council of your organisation was dubbed "The Twelve Apostles"?
(Note:- laughter in court.)
JP: That's correct. However I would like the court to know that I remain true to my background and upbringing. I am still, at least nominally, a Roman Catholic, albeit a very poor example of one. I am a sinner but I still pray to Mary Magdalena for forgiveness.
PM: I would have thought that a man like you would deal only with Almighty himself.
JP: I like to think I am a very humble man who is unfit to pray to The Almighty.
PM: "You just can't stop committing sins?"
(Note: There was no reply to this riposte by the Prosecutor and again there was laughter in court. The presiding judge warned everyone that a court was not a place for levity or ribaldry.)
PM: May I ask you to describe the procedure for meetings at the High Altar? Those in court will

bear in mind the warning about levity just issued by the presiding judge.

JP: Certainly. The Twelve Apostles would gather round the High Altar. It was a bit like the scene depicted in Da Vinci's Last Supper except that instead of having bread to break, the Twelve Apostles were always ordered to put their Glock pistols down on the altar where I could see them…

(Note: At this point in the proceedings there was hysterical laughter from the public gallery. Both men were ejected from the court on the instructions of the presiding judge. The judge warned everyone that any further disruption of proceedings would be dealt with severely and probably by imprisonment.)

PM: One of the witnesses has described how the commencement of one such meeting was interrupted by two members of the public calling at the front door?

JP: That is correct and I would like to tell the court how ashamed of myself I am. They were two old people who said that they wished to visit the Church in order to find closure over what had happened to them there as children. They said that they had been abused in the church as children by the clergy. I am deeply ashamed of what I said to them and apologise to them unreservedly. On that day I was dealing with one of The Apostles who had mislaid or stolen ten kilograms of cocaine at Schipol airport. I was in a state of some agitation and, I am ashamed to say-told the elderly couple to fuck off.

PM: What happened next?

JP: I returned to the High Altar to deal with Roberto, a Bolivian, who had lost or stolen the ten kilograms of cocaine. I think I called him a thieving Bolivian cunt...

(Note: There was further laughter in the public gallery and a man was taken into custody on the instructions of the presiding judge. As the man was taken away he was heard to shout that laughter in The Netherlands appeared to be a crime.)

PM: To round off this particular chapter in your evidence, one witness has averred that you had installed a springboard diving board in the pulpit and that you would punish those who disobeyed you or let you down by ordering that person to jump from the same.

JP: There was a diving board but I had it installed there as a joke. No-one was ever forced to jump from it.

JUDGE: Mr. Mondrian, I don't know about you but I have had enough for one day. The Court will be adjourned until tomorrow morning. Before rising from the bench, bring up that man from the cells who burst out laughing despite my explicit warnings. Someone go and find a lawyer not connected with this case. He will require representation. In fact he will require all the help he can get.

JUDGE: Good Morning, everyone. Mr Mondrian, please continue.

PM: There appears to be only one matter remaining, Senor Peron. There has been a suggestion in this case that you had a political agenda, that you saw yourself as some kind of latter-day Che. What would you to say about that matter?

JP: In the part of the world I come from Che has no shortage of admirers. Look, I am thirty-three years of age and have never taken part in political activity of any kind either here or anywhere else. I have no manifesto and no detailed political plans for the future. Yes, I have my dreams. But don't we all?

PM: Anything to add?

JP: No.

JUDGE: Thank you for giving your evidence. You will appear for sentence in this court next month on a day which the Clerk of Court will give you. The court is adjourned.

CHAPTER TWENTY FOUR
Statement given by a State Prosecutor on 8 October 2013

I am a State Prosecutor of The Kingdom of the Netherlands.

My position on this matter can be stated briefly. In May 2013 the police of Amsterdam made me aware that a girl was their custody in connection with her possession of a large uncut blue diamond on her arrival from South Africa.

In an effort no doubt to escape the consequences of her actions the girl provided the police with detailed information about an international drug smuggling ring whose "headquarters" were here in Amsterdam.

The size of the drug consignments was large as were the sums of money paid for them.

I gave appropriate directions in the case and numerous arrests were made here and in other countries including the man who was in charge of the ring-a certain Jesus Peron, a native of Peru and naturalised German citizen. His profession prior to that of making a career in crime was that of a doctor.

Those who were to stand were incarcerated here in Amsterdam. All were found guilty after trial.

On 4th October 2013 Jesus Peron was due to appear for sentence.

He did not appear and the circumstances of his non-appearance are described overleaf by the Governor of the prison.

CHAPTER TWENTY-FIVE
Sworn statement made by the Governor of the prison of Amsterdam to the State Prosecutor, the Kingdom of the Netherlands on 9 October 2013.

Sir,
I have been directed to report in writing on the results of my investigation into the "disappearance" of the prisoner Jesus Maria Magdalena Peron on the night or morning of 3rd 4th October 2013 from this penal establishment.

As you will know the prisoner Jesus Maria Magdalena Peron had been lodged in this establishment in late May 2013 pending his trial on major drug crimes. Having been found guilty on all counts, he was due to appear for sentence on the morning of 4th October 2013 at the central courts in Amsterdam.

At 6am on that morning prison officers attended at his cell with a view to rousing him and conveying him to the said courts there to be sentenced to a very lengthy period of imprisonment in respect of his crimes.

The prison officers found the cell empty and a Note left on the table addressed to myself.
It read:-
Dear Governor,
As you are well aware I am due for sentence today in the central courts. As you are also aware my first Christian name is Jesus (a common name in

Spanish custom). Having regard to the fact that my namesake was cruelly put to death 2000 years ago by the barbaric, Roman practice of crucifixion, I am disinclined to wait around for my own "crucifixion" set for this morning.
I have therefore ascended directly into Heaven with immediate effect.
I am but a humble sinner and drug smuggler with absolutely no religious powers. That said, I prayed nightly in my cell for forgiveness and early this morning, an Angel of the Lord together with Mary Magdalena appeared and said that God had sent them to pick me up. You may be interested to know, Dear Governor, that I asked both Holy Persons to check if Ernesto Che Guevara was already in Heaven. As I write this letter, both Holy Persons are making appropriate, urgent enquiries on their mobile phones.
I trust, dear Governor, that in the circumstances, you will forgive me for thus incommoding you by escaping from your delightful prison.
With warmest regards,
Jesus Maria Magdalena Peron.
PS Please show this letter to your superiors. It should exonerate you from incompetence."

Sir, no evidence whatsoever has been found of a break-in or for that matter a break-out at this establishment. All possible lines of enquiry are being pursued including advice from religious experts.
Signed,
Willem van der Waard,
Governor.

CHAPTER TWENTY SIX
Extract of a statement given to the police in Palma, Majorca on 11 October 2013 by Concepcion d...l...C....

My full name is Concepcion d...l...C... and I am 23 years of age having been born in the district of Steglitz, Berlin on 22 April 1990. I am the first cousin of Jesus Maria Magdalena Peron.
I have already made a lengthy statement to the authorities concerning the activities of Jesus Peron. I understand that he has escaped from prison leaving a letter for The Governor claiming that he has "ascended into heaven with immediate effect". If Jesus has escaped from prison leaving a letter for the Governor in such terms then it is entirely what I would expect from someone with his sense of humour.
I can only confirm, if such confirmation is required, that I saw no evidence in my dealings with my first cousin of any religious "powers" whatsoever. He was nominally a Roman Catholic but, as he himself was wont to say, a very poor example of one. He suffered merciless harassment at school in Berlin over his Christian names. His method of coping with that was to allude to the life and career of the Saviour. In adulthood the habit stuck. Later in Amsterdam and after he had acquired former church premises as office headquarters for his growing business enterprises, he continued to use

religious metaphors and analogies when describing phases in his own life.

I can confirm that he did have what might be called a "political agenda" but not in any conventional sense. It is fair to say that he hated what had happened to his own family in their native country. A brilliant medical career was never going to be enough for him. He sought to acquire vast sums of money to use as a basis for a future political career and, as he saw it, the liberation of his own people from the policies of the United States.

By any yardstick, he had not even begun a political career. As one of the mules has pointed out his ideas were nebulous and as yet inchoate.

As regards his "ascension into Heaven" or, far more likely, his escape from prison, I would, as a teacher, like to end my statement with a Latin proverb, **Quod erat demonstrandum.** The authorities may take what they wish out of that remark. Somewhat Delphic in the circumstances I know but I am not prepared to assist the authorities further.

For completeness, I am with child. Mmm. That sounds too biblical! I am pregnant. Jesus Peron is the father. Rudi was just a "useful fool" as Lenin would put it.

Lastly, has anyone given thought that Jesus Maria Magdalena may have been the Ant-Christ?

Oh dear, I see everyone is getting annoyed with me. The lips of one the policemen are trembling and the other policeman has made the Sign of the Cross! My lawyer has just whispered in my ear. He tells me to cut the funny stuff out.

Who says I am being funny?

**THE END
CHARLES J BUNYAN**

Herstellung und Verlag:
BoD – Books on Demand, Norderstedt
ISBN 978-3-7322-4183-5